1953

1953

Chronicle of a Birth Foretold

Translated by Robert Majzels

A Novel

France Daigle

Published in 1997 by
House of Anansi Press Limited
1800 Steeles Avenue West, Concord, ON
Canada L4K 2P3

First published in French as *1953:chronique d'une naissance annoncée* in 1995 by Les Éditions d'Acadie

Distributed in Canada by
General Distribution Services Inc.
30 Lesmill Road
Toronto, Canada M3B 2T6
Tel. (416) 445-3333
Fax (416) 445-5967
e-mail: Customer.Service@ccmailgw.genpub.com

Distributed in the United States by
General Distribution Services Inc.
85 River Rock Drive, Suite 202
Buffalo, New York 14207
Toll free 1-800-805-1083
Fax (416) 445-5967
e-mail: Customer.Service@ccmailgw.genpub.com

01 00 99 98 97   1 2 3 4 5

CATALOGUING IN PUBLICATION DATA
Daigle, France
[1953. English]
1953 : chronicle of a birth foretold
Translation of: 1953 : chronique d'une naissance annoncée
ISBN 0-88784-604-1
I. Majzels, Robert, 1950   . II. Title.   III. Title:
1953. English.   IV. Title: Nineteen fifty three.
PS8557.A423M5413 1997   C843'.54   C97-931854-8
PQ3919.2.D34M5413 1997

Text design: Tannice Goddard
Cover design: Pekoe Jones
Printed and bound in Canada
Typesetting: ECW Type & Art, Oakville

We acknowledge the support of the Canada Council for the Arts and the Ontario Arts Council for our publishing program.

This book was made possible in part through the Canada Council's Translation Grants Program.

To my mother and father

Contents

1953

Prologue

THE BALL RETURNS. Each ball is a challenge.

Whenever a story begins with a sports scene — which is quite common in films — there's a good chance the tale that follows is really about something completely different. This type of opening, which calls forth its subject gently and from a distance, is one of the conventions that have evolved over time between artists and their audience. The sports scene is not interpreted in a documentary sense; rather, it leads to something else. As a result, it has become something of a cliché. And, of course, unless deployed with finesse, clichés ought to be avoided. On the other hand, the fear of clichés ought not to lead us into the opposite error — just as tiresome in the long run — of originality at all costs, yet another trap for the artist. The author's problem.

And the ball returns.

This opening scene depicting a character — Brigitte in this case, momentarily overheated from the game — may or may not please. One may or may not enjoy this particular attempt at language, this manner of setting out to conquer meaning. Yet, independently of whether one likes or dislikes the scene, one senses that this deployment of physical force will be matched on a metaphysical level. Thus begins the activity in the reader-spectator's mind, the activity of understanding what ultimately will be signified by this image of Brigitte's body reacting like a machine to the ball which keeps coming back. In this search for meaning, the reader-spectator, like the person engrossed in her sport, is swept up in a game involving some difficulty and requiring a measure of skill, which are the bases of any exercise. One may like or dislike this. The reader's problem.

Each ball is a challenge.

The last time I sat down to write something resembling a novel, I began with a kind of longish discussion on the nesting habits of the American robin. One begins where one can. The gist of it was to establish whether spring had come sufficiently early to allow robins a second incubation period, thereby enriching the summer with two sets of fledglings. In the end, I dropped the chapter, which really had no place in the book. Since then, I have often wondered how I managed to completely excise a passage that, when I wrote it, seemed to go straight to the heart of the matter. Mere chatter? A volley of words because you have to start somewhere? Let's take another look at this chapter from *Real Life* entitled "Robins' Eggs":

For several days now, Élizabeth has noticed half-shells of a light blue colour scattered here and there over the neighbourhood sidewalks and flower beds. She knows they are robins' eggs because these are the only eggs she can recognize, aside from chicken and Easter eggs. Seeing them, her initial conclusion is that the nests must have been attacked by cats who, like buccaneers, tossed the still-warm eggs overboard. Élizabeth has always been wary of cats, and the discovery of the shells confirms this wariness. It does not occur to her that the chicks may already have dispensed with their shells. This seems impossible, since winter is barely over.

Élizabeth remained a long time bent over the first half-shell she found. The blue was very pale. Too pale. In fairness to the feline species, she questioned her initial reaction and admitted the possibility that the robin, having recognized, in its instinctive wisdom, a diseased egg, might have rejected it herself. Élizabeth was tempted to pick up the shell and keep it in the pocket of her coat, but she did not do so, for fear of crushing it inadvertently before the end of the day. She did, however, collect it that evening as she walked home from the hospital. She had the feeling it was somehow valuable. In the days that followed, she spotted several more of these pale blue shells. One had been crushed, stepped on maliciously, or so she suspected. A particle of down remained stuck to another. For a moment, Élizabeth had returned to her nest-wrecking theory, but then she had to admit that the down could have come from the brooder's abdomen.

Finally, after several days, and in spite of her incredulity, the abundance of shells had forced Élizabeth to conclude that the fledglings had, in fact, been born. Her gaze, which had been riveted on the ground, now rose up towards heaven and the trees, the image of a religious cliché which reminded her of Saint Francis of Assisi. But she neither saw nor heard anything new. She looked into the crook of a branch where a pair of robins had settled the previous year. Still nothing. Neither adult robins coming and going, sharing the duties of the nest, nor incessant cries emanating from tiny beaks pointed skyward. Élizabeth maintained her vigil a moment longer before continuing on her way to the hospital.

Élizabeth did not normally suffer from insomnia. Nevertheless, from time to time, she would wake suddenly during the night after several hours of deep sleep. Each time this happened she was surprised by the abruptness of the awakening. Each time, she had the feeling of passing instantly from black to white. Following one of these awakenings, in the pre-dawn darkness, she heard the insistent song of a robin whistling the same refrain over and over with as much conviction the twentieth time as the first. Other birds were singing in the distance. Some seemed to be replying. As she listened, Élizabeth was finally able to make out, somewhere nearer her window, a tiny choir actually echoing the robin. At that moment, she felt something extraordinary was happening. In fact, it seemed to her that the chicks were making a determined attempt to learn the robin's language by imitating its song. Élizabeth listened even more closely. Everything confirmed her initial impression. Could this be? She was well aware that her interpretations of life's events sometimes amused others. She was not offended. On the contrary, she was glad her interpretations served to disconcert, at least for a moment, the strict heel-and-toe of knowledge.

The little concert lasted a minute or two longer, after which the little ones, either drifting off-key or out of breath, were unable to complete the refrain. The adult robin made a few more attempts to lead them into song before abandoning the exercise. And in the ensuing silence, Élizabeth fell gently back to sleep, satisfied that the robin chicks were well and truly born, and happy to know that they had already begun to learn.

On the off-chance it might be relevant, I would like to add that I had intended the subsequent chapter to be entitled "i, as in Italy, or the paradoxical sleep."

The ball returns. Each ball is a challenge.

1

Celiac Trunk

Baby M. is admitted to the hospital — A disease of refusal — Style according to Roland Barthes — Nobel Prize in literature awarded to Winston Churchill — The politically dedicated man and the téléscripteur — The impact of the politically dedicated man and the téléscripteur on Nurse Vautour and Baby M.'s mother — Peristalsis and mother tongue according to Françoise Dolto — Chaos of continuity and silence of the organs — Nurse Vautour and the literary instinct — Marshal Tito's impertinence — Bananas for Czech children — Triumph of Personality over History

NURSE VAUTOUR is careful not to wake Baby M. as she lifts the child out of her mother's arms. The little one, who only moments ago was crying, has just fallen asleep. She's awfully pale and her dark-ringed eyes seem to have shrunk back into her head. In a few minutes, when Nurse Vautour changes Baby M.'s diaper for the first time, she will see her stomach, swollen and hard as a ball. The bulging stomach contrasts sharply with the rest of Baby M.'s body: the rump and thighs almost bare of fat, the groin wrinkled as an old man's skin.

As she places her child in the arms of the nurse, Baby M.'s mother can't help but feel relieved that someone else is taking over. But this feeling is really only a manifestation of her confusion, for Baby M.'s mother has never had such a sick child. And yet, she has lavished the same care on Baby M. as on the four children that preceded her, all of whom are in fine health. True, in the beginning, she was not seriously worried by Baby M.'s lack of appetite. It is not uncommon for a child to balk at its food. Later, after Baby M. had vomited several times, her mother more or less concluded it was a virus, some sort of temporary illness. But the persistence of the child's profuse and nauseating diarrhea had seriously perplexed her. Finally, the doctor's diagnosis confirmed the strangeness of the phenomenon.

In the early 1950s, little was known about the cause of celiac disease, also called intestinal infantilism or idiopathic sprue. In spite of this, the once fatal disease had been reclassified as curable, conditional on the scrupulous maintenance of a strict diet. Not only did this dietary treatment increase the success rate for the treatment of celiac children, but it also refuted the theory that the origin of the disease was psychic. Indeed, many doctors and researchers believed that celiac disease was a psychological illness based on refusal. They pointed to the absence of any expression of joy or pleasure in the faces of celiac children, who tend to concentrate all their attention on themselves rather than on the surrounding objects or people.

As she takes Baby M. from the arms of her mother, Nurse

Vautour can't help but share the feeling that she has never seen such a sick child. Baby M.'s tiny sunken eyes, squeezed tightly shut, her tiny, ethereal, almost lifeless body, go straight to Nurse Vautour's heart. On one level, she can't bear this suffering, and yet, she is gripped by a kind of desperate love for the situation. As Baby M. passes into her arms, something which Nurse Vautour cannot name transpires, something like a veil falling and draping over life, over all life, and propelling, as it falls, Nurse Vautour into its orbit.

℀

The celiac trunk is an arterial trunk attached to the aorta at the level of the twelfth dorsal vertebra. Part of the celiac plexus (which extends from the solar plexus), the celiac trunk measures from one to three centimetres and is composed of three terminal branches. It carries the arterial blood to the liver, the stomach, the great omentum, the spleen and, to some degree, the pancreas. The celiac trunk resembles, therefore, the thousands of systems or organizations which more or less make the world go round, including hospitals for the sick and a host of other achievements of civilization. As evidenced by Baby M.'s medical file, the Hôtel-Dieu de l'Assomption Hospital of Moncton was part and parcel of this fabulous universe of organization. One learns from the aforementioned document, drawn from archives which constitute further proof of the splendour of this organization that, with the exception of a few undoubtedly well-earned days off, two nurses, relaying each other virtually night and day, tended to Baby M. during her three-week stay in the hospital. Nurse Vautour lavished her care and monitored Baby M.'s antics during the day, while her colleague Nurse Comeau watched over the child at night.

Baby M.'s treatment was essentially the same throughout her stay in the hospital: injections in the buttocks, feedings, baths. In their daily notes, Nurse Vautour and Nurse Comeau reported the degree of distension and hardness of the abdomen, and the consistency of the stool. They noted that the child was not difficult, that she seemed happy to drink and eat, and that she slept peacefully. From time to time she cried. Nevertheless, the statement "little change" returns like a refrain at the close of almost all their periodic observations, giving the lie to the quasi-angelic behaviour of Baby M. who, meanwhile, continued to grind her food to death and expel it without the slightest restraint. This extraordinary diarrhea is really just the final phase of the disease's process, which begins we know not where, per-haps in the pancreas, perhaps in the liver, perhaps in the stomach. Or perhaps in the brain, in the area where refusal speaks. And indeed, the mystery of the cause of celiac disease compels Nurse Vautour and Nurse Comeau to tend to the spirit of Baby M. as much as to her body. Nurse Vautour is especially sensitive to this. Each time she swad-dles Baby M., she is thinking as much about her soul as her body. In fact, she always washes Baby M. with special care, taking the time to cuddle her and whisper words which, at the time, were snatched from eternity, but have long since been returned to it.

☙

And while Baby M. continued to remain impermeable to the nutrients so essential to her survival, Roland Barthes was writing, in *Writing Degree Zero*, that "language is a kind of natural ambience wholly pervading the writer's expression, yet without endowing it with form or content: it is, as it were, an abstract circle of truths, outside of which alone the solid residue of an individual *logos* begins to settle." Furthermore, he added, "imagery, delivery, vocabulary spring from the body and the past of the writer and gradually become the very reflexes of his art. . . . Its frame of reference is biological or biographical, not historical," the writer's style nothing more than "the decorative voice of hidden, secret flesh; it works as does Necessity, as if, in this kind of floral growth, style were no more than the outcome of a blind and stubborn metamorphosis starting from a sublanguage elaborated where flesh and external reality come together."

As, once more, she confronts the language of Baby M., Nurse Vautour is unaware that she is changing the diaper and washing the bottom of a writer. She does not suspect that her hands are immersed in a budding literature. She cannot appreciate, at their just merits, the nuances in the yellows, greens, and greys of the excrement, not to mention its greasy textures, its frequency, and its stench. Nurse Vautour is not thinking about literature. She is thinking about life, Baby M.'s life in particular, while the latter seems as indifferent as ever to the fact that life might escape her at any moment, might slip away, take another route, take root elsewhere. She searches for the thread by which to draw the child back to life. The doctor has ordered that Baby M. be fed bananas. Nurse Vautour proffers bananas. And more bananas.

Nurse Vautour does not think of herself as someone who knows much about literature. In fact, literature is something

Nurse Vautour does not think about. Not directly anyway. Nevertheless, she does sense in Baby M. an inclination towards inaccessibility, a semblance of camouflage. She senses Baby M. is merely circling around the disease rather than plunging straight into it. Which explains the difficulty of breaking the child's stagnant condition. On the other hand, Nurse Vautour also believes something holds Baby M. to life. She thinks this something could be the disease itself, as though, for Baby M., the illness were a sort of positive attraction, a door into life. Whereas for most people, disease is a way out, for Baby M. it could be a way in. And so Nurse Vautour is alert to other signs which might demonstrate Baby M.'s intention to cross the threshold to life. And she makes every effort to give Baby M. the opportunity to demonstrate that intention. But the days pass and still nothing. Baby M. accepts the food she is offered, submits to the injections, sleeps quietly most of the time, allows herself to be wrapped and rocked, but she refuses to give in to life. She keeps life imprisoned beneath the dome of her hard, round belly, only releasing it after long slow ruminations punctuated by excrement as formless as it is fetid.

Nurse Vautour's intuition concerning Baby M. is not unlike Barthes's, according to whom "style is properly speaking a germinative phenomenon, the transmutation of a Humour . . . a secret . . . locked within the body of the writer." It's probably a good thing that Nurse Vautour did not read *Writing Degree Zero* at the time of its publication. She might have found it impudent of Baby M. to hijack medicine in this way for literary purposes. Was it really necessary to go through so much in order to be born to literature? In any case, even if she had read the book, Nurse Vautour lacked the necessary distance to see the bigger picture. Celiac disease, or intestinal infantilism, or idiopathic sprue, was simply one of the components of this writer's body circling in the orbit of her eternal subject "above History as the freshness of Innocence."

છ

In 1953, the Western world witnessed another great literary moment, aside from the publication of Roland Barthes's *Writing Degree Zero.* That year, the Nobel Prize in literature was awarded to none other than the legendary champion of the Second World War, British Prime Minister Winston Churchill. The decision to award the Nobel Prize to the renowned cigar smoker was not, however, universally acclaimed. Many felt that the Nobel Prize in literature ought to celebrate the contributions of a fiction writer rather than those of a historical or biographical champion. A number of people were, therefore, less than enthusiastic about the awarding of this prize of literary prizes to Mr. Churchill. Some even felt the members of the Swedish Academy of Letters had bungled badly, mistaking Personality for History itself.

Indeed, Winston Leonard Spencer Churchill is as open to multiple interpretations as is Literature or History. His flamboyant personality certainly had something to do with the comment by one critic, in 1923, that he had written "an enormous work on himself" and entitled it *The World Crisis.* At the time, Churchill was close to fifty years old. He had already straddled two centuries and a world war. The future "driving force" of the Second World War had already demonstrated that he possessed an "artist's taste for war," that "he had never been attracted to lost causes," and that "he had never felt himself unprepared for any task." When he was awarded the Nobel Prize in literature, in the fall of 1953, he was preparing to celebrate his seventy-ninth birthday. A birthday which, as a matter of fact, happened to fall on the same day as Baby M.'s mother's.

In his book *Winston Churchill and Twentieth-Century England*, the French historian Jacques Chastenet speaks of the "Churchillian childhoods" to evoke the complexity of the character, no doubt because a single childhood could not easily have contained the enormous legacy on the paternal side — two centuries of British warriors and statesmen — and, on the maternal side, an American blood-line streaming with New York celebrities and even a few drops of Iroquois. Lady Randolph Churchill, born Jenny Jerome, could trace her American roots back to the beginning of the eighteenth century. Her father, Leonard Jerome, had, in addition, acquired the *New York Times*. He was a man with a passion for horses, a collector of fine art, and a patron of the theatre. No surprise then to find the grandson Winston, during the lean years of his political and military career, engaged in painting and writing.

The Nobelization of Winston Churchill followed that of François Mauriac in 1952, a French-Catholic novelist who was also a playwright, biographer, poet, and journalist. The Nobel Committee of the Swedish Academy of Letters had noted the spiritual depth and artistic intensity of Mauriac's semi-autobiographical novels, novels which depicted Man torn between the forces of good and evil, between the weakness of the flesh and the lofty aspirations of the spirit. Winston Churchill, for his part, had summed himself up as follows: "I am a very simple man, but the best in the world is not too good for me!" The Nobelization of Churchill was followed, in 1954, by that of the American Ernest Hemingway, hailed for his powerful mastery of narrative, as displayed in *The Old Man and the Sea*. Although it was at first critical of the brutality and cynicism of his early work, the Swedish Academy was won over by the "heroic pathos" of Hemingway's writing, along with his "manly love of danger and adventure." Finally, the jury of the Nobel Prize in literature praised the ex-journalist's natural admiration for those who battle on the side of good in a universe clouded by violence and death. For Churchill, who loved life, war was a form of life, though he despised the unnecessary spilling of blood.

ℰℐ

The omnipresence of journalism in the careers of Mauriac, Churchill, and Hemingway, to mention only these, should not surprise us. In the chapter "Political Modes of Writing" in *Writing Degree Zero*, Roland Barthes explains that "the spreading influence of political and social facts into the literary field of consciousness has produced a new type of scriptor, halfway between the party member and the writer, deriving from the former an ideal image of committed man, and from the latter the notion that a written work is an act." The grouping of the words *new type of scriptor* actually brings to mind the French word *téléscripteur*, "teletyper" in English, that almost-infernal machine which used to spit up a continuous stream of dispatches in every newsroom. It just so happens that Baby M.'s father was one of that new type of scriptor. The act, in his case, consisted in doing his utmost to ensure the daily publication of *l'Évangéline*, the newspaper that provided Acadians with a link to the nerve centres of the world. His mission was not in vain. Nurse Vautour, for example, read *l'Évangéline* every morning before setting out for the hospital. After quickly scanning the headlines, she would plunge into the column "Around the World," a collection of news reports on a smattering of events of varying importance. It was more or less on the basis of this column that Nurse Vautour composed her own overall portrait of humanity. And her opinion of humanity was pretty much settled by the time she took Baby M. in her arms, at the moment of the latter's birth, in 1953. Nor had her world view changed much by the time Baby M. returned to the hospital for her celiac stay, in 1954. For Nurse Vautour too, the die was cast; all that remained was to digest the results.

Baby M. was thus born at the moment when this digestive work was beginning. Already, her gestation period had been highly active, including a string of grand and noble ceremonies. The month of January set the tone for the entire year. Baby M. who, though not yet conceived, already existed in the form of an inescapable probability, was thus witness to the fulfilment of Pope Pius XII's dream of completing the Sacred College of Cardinals, something which the sixteen popes who had succeeded Clement XI in the early eighteenth century had failed to accomplish. During the approximately 250 years of the Sacred College's existence, death had constantly intervened to create vacancies among the seventy seats of the plenum created by Sixtus V in 1585 in memory of the seventy elders gathered by Moses to govern the people of Israel. The consistory was therefore called by Pius XII to promote twenty-four eminencies to the rank of cardinal, thereby filling that same number of empty places. The consistory itself was held behind closed doors for several days, but it concluded with "a ceremony unprecedented throughout the world for its splendour and pomp." Sixteen of the new cardinals, among them the archbishop of Montréal, Mgr. Paul-Émile Léger, were appointed Princes of the Church before a crowd of forty thousand, who began by watching the sovereign pontiff as he was carried on his gestatorial chair from one end of St. Peter's Basilica to the other. Later, the new cardinals, "dressed in crimson robes bordered in ermine," humbly prostrated themselves beneath the dome of the Vatican Basilica, while the papal choir sang "Te es Petrus." Also on parade were "the noble guards in shining helmets, the Swiss guards carrying their sixteenth century halberds, the Palatine guards in dark blue uniform with gold buttons and the pontifical men-at-arms in their variegated dress." At various moments during the ceremony, the new cardinals took their oaths, kneeled with heads bowed to the ground, kissed the hand of the pope, and received the pontiff's accolade (the first bishop of India to wear the crimson was held a moment longer than the others in His Holiness's embrace). One after the other, the new Princes of the Church approached Pius XII to receive "the third of their three distinct red hats, the large-bordered galéro, adorned with thirty egret feathers," the red symbolizing the blood they were prepared to shed in defence of their faith.

As sumptuous as were the closing ceremonies of the consistory, they were rapidly surpassed by the swearing-in of Dwight David Eisenhower as president of the United States. The inauguration was televised, for the first time, across the entire United States, which meant that up to seventy million people watched Eisenhower succeed Harry

Truman. The new president naturally took advantage of the broadcast's extraordinary range to clear up a thing or two. In a powerful presidential speech, Eisenhower announced the United States' determination to confront the Communist threat "with confidence and conviction," while extending a hand to all (even Communist) nations that aspired to a relaxation of tensions in the world. Not once during his entire speech did the president utter the words *Russia* or *Communist*, managing instead to deliver his message by referring only to the forces of good and evil, a clever stratagem which was widely noted at the time.

Speaking of evil, Stalin died two months after Eisenhower's inaugural speech. Judging from the grandiose funeral which took place on Red Square, Communist fervour was not about to die with him. As for the funeral of Queen Mary (the late George V of England's consort, who also died in March of 1953, a few weeks after Stalin), it was relatively modest if one considers the scope of her life, which stretched from the era of lances and sabres to the atomic age. In June, however, the British deployed all their festive skills for the coronation of Elizabeth II. From the start of the year, this event had been gathering daily momentum across the Empire. *L'Évangéline* also reflected the Anglo fever, just as it had described the reverberations emanating first from Rome, then Washington and Moscow. Baby M., who observed all this from the comfort of the uterus, later incorporated these emanations into her intra- and extra-uterine development, particularly at the moment of separation from her mother and initiation into desire (desire for the mother in the first place, then desire for language), as well as at the moment of differentiating between needs and desires, and in a general way, during the entire period of construction of the body as a site of security. As pointed out by the pediatrician and psychoanalyst Françoise Dolto in *Solitude*, this structuring of the child passes necessarily through the awareness of her personal digestive tube.

☙

Unlike Roland Barthes, Françoise Dolto does not deal specifically with literature when she tackles the question of style, arguing that "each mother, unbeknownst to her . . . gives her child her style." In fact, she writes of the joy and sadness associated with the realm of existential security, a realm which is closely tied to the mother's gestural and expressive language, and inseparable from the mother's reactions to her child's defecation. Thus, for example, if a mother "cannot bear the smell, if she takes it away too quickly and fails to speak cheerfully of the attention the baby sometimes elicits deliberately, then, because it is rejected by her mother, the child's own body becomes the enemy," which has the effect of weakening the fundamental narcissistic structure of the child. Madame Dolto also adds that the peristalsis from the mouth to the anus is synony- mous, to the child, with the presence of the mother within. This explains why we human beings know "at all times where the mother's presence is located within us, in the form of the partial object which comes from her [food] and which we return to her [excrement]." The absence of this "intuitive sensation of existence" at the level of the digestive tube is a source of anxiety.

At the same time, Madame Dolto is careful to point out another essential contribution of the mother: that of inciting the child to actively seek out communication. According to her, the child is capable of hearing and producing "all the phonemes of every language in the world . . . But, very quickly, its mouth will lose this ability . . . because it seeks to perpetuate the presence of the mother." The child works, therefore, at producing "the lallations and phonemizations that echo, in an acoustic mirror . . . the sounds of the language spoken by its mother." In other words, the desire to communicate through language is directly linked to the desire for the mother, and the transmission of the mother tongue is an offshoot of this initial experience of desire. In that sense, *l'Évangéline*, printed daily on an old rotary press (purchased, as a matter of fact, from the *New York Times*) provided both the evidence and the continuation of the attachment of Acadians to their mother. And, if the paper's editorial board was not aware of accomplishing a mission dictated by desire, it was fully conscious of the importance of the role of the Acadian mother. This explains the frequency with which she was evoked in the pages of that paper. As evidence, an excerpt from a speech by an American priest, who argued that the true Catholic mother is, at one and the same time, "nurse, prioress, educator, martyr, and queen," and cannot but be our inspiration, because she "approaches things and people from the point of view of eternity."

એ

From Madame Dolto's work, two essential notions emerge: the idea of continuity (continuity of peristalsis from the mouth to the anus) and the idea of consciousness (the baby's consciousness of this activity in its digestive tract). So ingrained in the human psyche is the notion of continuity that it would be ridiculous for any human being to attempt to abandon it. Nor is it even certain that we succeed in doing so in death. The deep roots of the notion of continuity become more apparent when one reflects on its opposite: the idea of discontinuity, which immediately evokes a profoundly disagreeable sense of chaos and absurdity. Imagine, for example, your reaction on learning that the production of parts for the car you purchased only a year ago had been discontinued. Humanity lives in the certitude that the present follows the past and leads to the future. All these concepts — the progression of History; the relation between cause and effect, and between our acts and their consequences; the linear movement of time — are only a few of the manifestations of the principle of continuity. Although the principle of continuity provides only a partial explanation of the origin and ultimate meaning of humanity, most people manage to coexist quite comfortably with the remaining mysteries. By compartmentalizing their experiences and identifying a few cycles, people manage to live moderately happy lives without understanding the truth of the matter and without seriously questioning their sense of History.

In the same way, we humans are perfectly capable of conceiving of any number of things without necessarily possessing sufficient knowledge to act on these concepts. For example, one can easily imagine a fish without being able to manufacture one. In fact, simply catching a fish requires considerable cunning. Yet another case of mind over matter. Reality is such that human beings can taste the simple pleasures of life without being burdened by the details of all that lies beneath the surface. Consider, for example, the non-linearity of continuity. The way continuity advances simultaneously on several fronts, in several, and even opposite, directions. Because continuity does not develop in a long gradual wave, born and dying in the ocean of History. It also develops in shocks and sudden jolts, the way, when it rains, a multitude of rings collides on the water's surface. This chaos of continuity exists in that invisible and indivisible part of History where even History loses consciousness of itself. The chaos of continuity exists at the nuclear level, hence its true mystery and its incomparable strength.

As for consciousness, Françoise Dolto explains that the sensation of existence derived from the child's peristalsis is a sensation which is not perceived. According to her, we all live with this imperceptible sensation, the exception being those suffering from extreme anxiety, people who, for the most part, are restricted to psychiatric hospitals and claim to have neither stomachs nor intestines. In the words of Madame Dolto, "the fact that there are those that imagine the absence of the body proves that everyone always feels they have a stomach, always feels they have a digestive canal, which is in continuous peristalsis. How it operates, they have no idea. This unconscious sensation . . . is part of the silence of the organs." Lack of consciousness, in this case, is therefore a healthy sign. Consciousness (that of a novelist reflecting on his or her art, for example) might then be interpreted as an anomaly. Transposing further, one might assume that a silence corresponding to the "silence of the organs" exists in other spheres of life and that, similarly, a relative lack of consciousness is preferable to an over-sharp mind, assuming we accept as a worthwhile human objective to stay as far away as possible from psychiatric institutions. It follows that the silence of continuity which underlies everything (including chaos) could be part of the human condition, that is, of that part of the condition which it would be preferable to forget. Because one form or another of insanity threatens anyone who is unable to forget that life — which is really nothing more than a long succession of endlessly repeating stories containing neither anything new nor anything we can change — is, in the end, futile.

࿔

Nineteen fifty-three turned out to be a rather emotional year for Winston Churchill, in spite of the fact that, during this post-war period, he was responsible for only a single country's destiny, which, for him, was not a lot. In fact, during the years following the Second World War, the Great Britain in Churchill's hands looked more like a trifle in the grip of a giant. Nevertheless, like all Personalities, he always found a way to remain on the cusp of History. In the early days of 1953, even before Pius XII's consistory and Eisenhower's swearing-in ceremony, but not prior to the inescapable probability of Baby M.'s existence, Churchill once again made himself known to History, by dealing this time with his own history. At seventy-nine years of age, Mr. Churchill visited for the first time his mother's birthplace in Brooklyn. Jenny Jerome had been born in a small brownstone, in 1851, a century earlier. This modest pilgrimage, a brief stopover on the way to Jamaica, was enough to stir many hearts in the international community and set Nurse Vautour to dreaming whether she too would one day visit New York and — why not? — Brooklyn.

Unlike Mr. Churchill, Nurse Vautour has no conception of

her role in the continuity of History nor, for that matter, in the continuity of Literature. Unaware of the literary instinct hidden away in Baby M.'s celiac trunk, it is with thoughts of the continuity of life, more particularly Baby M.'s, that Nurse Vautour once again takes the baby in her arms to give her a bath. The fact that Baby M. does not really look any better reminds her that humankind in general is not doing very well either; otherwise, the world would not be so full of spies and saboteurs like the Rosenbergs, God forgive them! All those atomic secrets, it's very unsettling; no wonder the Nevada desert is trembling. Truman and Eisenhower have said so: the hydrogen bomb will certainly destroy Russia and the Reds, but not without wiping out the entire planet as well. All things considered, the world is an uncertain place. The Russians claim they are victims of a vast American anti-Communist propaganda, and Charlie Chaplin, that benevolent clown, agrees. But Nurse Vautour believes one should not underestimate the Reds' impertinence either. Marshall Tito, for example, has not even taken the trouble to read Pope Pius XII's letters, which call on him to put an end to the persecution of Catholics in his country. Instead, the Yugoslavian leader returned the letters unopened to the Vatican. Having emerged once more from Baby M.'s celiac cloud, Nurse Vautour hopes something good will come of all this. She thinks of the Japanese scientists who have invented a new cyclotron, which could serve the cause of medicine. Canadians too have reason to be proud. In Chalk River, they've constructed a unit in which the body of a cancer patient can be entirely surrounded by radioactive cobalt. Even the Americans have expressed an interest. Nurse Vautour wonders whether some such technique might not work on Baby M., because the banana potions don't seem to be having much of an effect. She recalls a newsflash in *l'Évangéline* about how a great number of Czech children, who had never seen a banana in their lives, were each given one for Christmas.

As for the awarding of the Nobel Prize in literature to Mr. Churchill, Nurse Vautour received the news without much fuss — by now, she has become accustomed to a state of perpetual surprise. In fact, she was surprised mainly that, with all his worldly concerns, Mr. Churchill had found the time to write books. The awarding of the prize to Mr. Churchill made little impact in the mass media. It was a less-than-memorable Nobel Prize, compared to Mauriac's or Hemingway's, for example, whose names and work have left a greater mark on the literary landscape. No doubt, we ought to reread the writings of Winston Churchill to remind ourselves of his qualities as a man of letters. We might find in him a precursor of the mise en abîme so dear to postmodern literature (Mr. Churchill having written "an enormous work on himself" and having entitled it *The World Crisis*). Perhaps he should be rehabilitated, as the Communists he so detested would say (it was Mr. Churchill who first coined the phrase *the iron curtain*). As for the members of the Nobel Committee of the Swedish Academy, their 1953 selection may correspond to one of those imperceptible moments of continuity in which Literature, having lost a measure of self-consciousness, momentarily lets slip the barriers that habitually separate the novelist from his characters, and the novel from History.

2

Death of Stalin

Man of steel falls to hardening of the arteries and into coma — Exposition in the grand Hall of the Trade Unions — The Antichrist who despised family life — Illness and death of Queen Mary — The Duke of Windsor's grief at his mother Queen Mary's funeral — Talent for evasion and problem of truth — Language and truth — Language and humanity — Return of Corporal Maillet of Lewisville — Baby M.'s mother and Nurse Vautour are dissatisfied — The Boston Braves move to Milwaukee

BABY M.'s MOTHER and Nurse Vautour learned of Stalin's death in *l'Évangéline* on Friday, March 6, 1953. The leader of the Communist world had passed away the previous evening, in Moscow. The man of steel's right side had been paralysed by a cerebral hemorrhage, which had subsequently caused a coma. Kremlin doctors had battled in vain against the hardening of the arteries. Death, supreme, had finally come between their comrade and his work.

Nevertheless, even as the Soviet authorities announced that "the heart of the comrade and brilliant perpetuator of Lenin's will, the chief sage and master of the Communist Party and Soviet people, Joseph Vissarionovich Stalin, had ceased to beat," it was clear that the flame of the Bolshevik revolution was not yet extinguished.

Nurse Vautour and the woman in whose womb Baby M. had begun to take shape followed with some interest the funeral of the Number One Red. His body lay in state in the grand Hall of the Trade Unions, five minutes from the Kremlin, in the heart of Moscow. During the first night, between Friday and Saturday, more than a million people filed past the casket. In the few days that followed, five million people came to pay their last respects to their leader, who was dressed in his marshall's uniform with its sole decoration, while his medals were displayed on red silk cushions nearby. Soldiers stood guard next to the casket surrounded by flowers, while orchestras played sad songs and works by Tchaïkovsky and Glinka, the deceased's favourite composers.

That Monday, "following a profound silence," the remains of the Soviet leader were laid to rest "in a tomb of red and black marble . . . a magnificent art object," while the cannons of Moscow and twenty-three other great Soviet cities boomed, and the Kremlin's bells tolled. Earlier, the comrades of the new leadership had lifted "the velvet-trimmed casket onto their shoulders" to carry it down "to the gun carriage" while "hundreds of musicians, their instruments wrapped in black ribbons," had taken up Chopin's funeral march. Among the eight pallbearers were Stalin's successor, Georgi Malenkov, as well as Vyacheslav Molotov, Lavrenti Beria, and Nikita Khrushchev. In spite of a glacial wind, millions of citizens lined the snow-covered streets of the capital to greet the procession. Millions of flowers (red and white roses, tulips, narcissi, and mimosas) had been brought in from the warmer climes of the USSR to decorate Red Square and the walls of the buildings along the funeral route. As had been done with Lenin, Stalin's body was embalmed according to a secret process perfected by Russian scientists, in order to preserve his features so that they could be viewed by future generations.

Nor were Baby M.'s mother and Nurse Vautour indifferent to the consequences of Stalin's death. They were well aware of the general concern over the continuation of History, particularly since it seemed that Stalin had been at the helm of the impenetrable Soviet Union forever. Georgi Malenkov, who wanted to prove himself worthy of the task which had fallen to him, made his maiden speech at the funeral service of the man whom he was succeeding. As he spoke, "Malenkov was bare-headed, and obviously under an enormous emotional strain. From time to time, he passed a hand over his eyes, as though he were wiping tears spawned by his grief or perhaps by the wind that whipped the funeral decorations." Having declared that "the Party, the Soviet people, the entire human race had suffered a terrible and irreparable loss," he proclaimed Stalin "humanity's greatest genius." Malenkov also took upon himself the sacred duty of carrying on Stalin's peace plan, which included a meeting with President Eisenhower. After detailed study of the funeral orations by Malenkov, Beria (Minister of the Interior), and Molotov (Minister of External Affairs), Western diplomats concluded that the Soviet leadership would continue to advocate peaceful coexistence between the capitalist and socialist camps.

&

In spite of their reservations about the fearsome conqueror, Western nations sent messages of sympathy and condolence to the grieving Russian people. The premier of Québec, Maurice Duplessis, did less than anyone to conceal his true feelings. He hailed the death of the Communist leader by declaring that Stalin "had all the characteristics of an Antichrist." This categorical stance was echoed widely in scarcely couched terms by the Western press. The following comment, for example, was in many ways typical: "Stalin transformed Russia into a major industrial power, stopping at nothing in order to achieve his goal of domination through world Communism. Every human value was violated under his reign. He kept the entire world on alert, only to suffer in the end the common mortal's fate."

Baby M.'s mother and Nurse Vautour had difficulty understanding how a carpenter's son had risen to absolute mastery over eight hundred million people without demonstrating at least a trace of goodness. They therefore read every article in *l'Évangéline* about this mysterious man. They learned that Stalin had been an erudite and shrewd political scientist who had established "a system of incredible horror" which was, nevertheless, efficient and productive. He was also described as an "impassive and extremely taciturn man . . . who could be affable and take on the mantle of a true father toiling for his family." But it would be a mistake to fall for such posing, because Stalin "had always despised family life." In fact, both of his marriages had ended badly, and his son Vassily, a pilot, was known "to regularly spend vast sums of money on parties with lovely young ladies." This spendthrift son was something of a paradox, since

Stalin himself "seemed to have maintained his typically Marxist contempt for personal wealth." Stalin was also widely denounced for conducting his business at night and for consuming immense quantities of vodka.

❧

L'Évangéline published a detailed account of Stalin's funeral the day after the lavish ceremony of Monday, March 9, 1953. On the same day, in the "Around the World" column, there appeared a brief item on the health of Mary, queen consort of the deceased George V. At the age of eighty-five, Elizabeth II's grandmother had been suffering from a gastric illness that had kept her in bed for close to two weeks. Doctors had declared her condition satisfactory, but the situation was delicate due to the "indomitable dowager's" advanced age. Less than a fortnight later, she was dead. The queen consort passed away in a peaceful sleep, during the evening of March 24, in her palace at Marlborough. The archbishop of Canterbury and the royal family were at her bedside. Prime Minister Churchill announced the demise of Queen Mary in the Commons, an hour after her death. He immediately adjourned the Chamber's session "in order to mourn this proud and fine lady who had dedicated her life to her country."

If the figure of Stalin was the incarnation of the formidable power of the Communist advance, Queen Mary served as the representative of the so-called free peoples of the world. Messages of condolence poured in from everywhere, that is, from every corner of the Empire, as well as from independent nations of democratic tradition, and they were unanimous: Queen Mary was admired for her goodness, her kindness, and her benevolent influence. Even Baby M.'s father weighed in with a brief but respectful editorial, noting that this was not the time to discuss the significance of the British monarchy for French Canada. Under the title "A queen leaves this world," he summed up the situation as follows: "For more than a century, the Heavens seem to have favoured the throne of England with an outpouring of respect which we would be hard put to contradict. While, in other lands, princes have been the brunt of contempt, Queen Mary has maintained the mantle of a great lady, always poised, generous, and courageous. And when one considers the respect in which the royal family generally continues to be held, Queen Mary can be said to have been an educator who remained faithful to her duty. She lived to see her fourth generation, which is the Church's pronounced wish for all newlyweds, as a reward for those who remain faithful to their condition in life. In our topsy-turvy world, the dignity of kings offers hope for the final triumph of a social order in which each of us accepts his or her role with equal dignity."

Over the centuries, the high regard in which the British people held their royal family had been somewhat diminished by a host of unfortunate incidents. George V and his wife, Mary, who ruled together from 1910 until the king's death in 1936, had shown themselves to be worthy of the respect mentioned by the editor of *l'Évangéline*. George V was a man "of good sense, dedicated to his duties." After his death, Queen Mary maintained her husband's democratic and constitutional attitude. Her reputation also profited from the heroism of her son George VI, who had won the hearts of his subjects by refusing to flee to the safety of the countryside when the bombs rained down on London during the Second World War. At the moment of Queen Mary's death, the British people, barely recovered from the passing of brave George VI a year earlier, had put their trust in his daughter Elizabeth, who had already begun to symbolize the unity and continuity of the Empire. Indeed, *l'Évangéline*'s article announcing Queen Mary's death had made a point of evoking this principle of continuity by pointing out that "Queen Elizabeth II, who ordinarily was due a curtsy from the dowager, had knelt in a gesture of love and respect for her grandmother at whose knee she had learned the rudiments of a sovereign's duties."

What most impressed Baby M.'s mother and Nurse Vautour about Queen Mary's funeral was the display of emotion by the Duke of Windsor, the black sheep of the royal family. According to *l'Évangéline*, the queen's "favourite son" cried throughout the entire private ceremony, which was conducted in the presence of four queens, two kings, and several other members of the "declining aristocracy of Europe," in Windsor Castle's St. George Chapel. The two Acadians were shocked to see, in black and white, that a mother — and a queen to boot — had admitted to a preference for one of her children. They wondered if this sort of confession was acceptable among Protestants, or whether it was perhaps a way for the royal family to remind the world that they were, after all, only human. Because the truth was that this particular "favourite son's" tastes were not in keeping with the standards of the monarchy; he had even been obliged to abdicate the throne in order to marry the woman he loved. For the mothers of the time and their derivatives (such as nurses, prioresses, educators, martyrs, and queens), this was *l'Évangéline*'s real soap opera, rather than the "Cry of the Banshee," a serialized novel with a pseudo-exotic title, which provided far less excitement than the royal heartbreaks of the House of Windsor.

છ

In his memoirs, Hitler's minister of foreign affairs, Joachim von Ribbentrop, affirms that Hitler secretly admired Stalin, his political foe. According to Ribbentrop, who was hanged at Nuremberg for his war crimes, Hitler dreamed of capturing Stalin. The Führer would have granted him a luxurious asylum in a German castle. We can only imagine what security precautions Hitler would have put in place to keep his guest from slipping through his fingers, in light of Stalin's well-known talent for evasion. As evidence of this ability, consider that Stalin was not even the real name of this serpentine personage. The son of a relatively poor family from Gori, a suburb of Tiflis, the capital of Georgia, he had been baptized Iosif Vissarionovich Dzhugashvili. Though they were poor, his parents had promised him to the priesthood of the Greek Orthodox Church. As a matter of fact, it was in the seminary that young Joseph developed a taste for revolutionary socialism. He quickly demonstrated his leadership qualities — much too quickly, in the opinion of the priests, who soon expelled the undesirable politician. It was not long after his expulsion that Stalin opted to become a professional revolutionary. He was a member of one of the first cells of the Bolshevik party, worked under Lenin's leadership and, like a typical Russian revolutionary, was arrested and shipped off to the salt mines of Siberia. And yet, "in less than a month, he was back in Tiflis with a new name and a new haircut. He was later arrested, imprisoned, and exiled, and escaped half a dozen times under as many different names. The last of these names was Stalin, and he kept it."

Stalin, the man of steel, quickly rose to the sixth or seventh rank of leadership in the ongoing revolutionary movement. He had, among other things, led the Bolshevik group that seized power in Petrograd in 1917. Supreme power, however, remained in the hands of Lenin, who was able to control the internal jealousies and struggles which might have harmed the party. Among these threats was the conflict between Stalin and Trotsky. In the end, from his deathbed, in 1924, Lenin judged Stalin too impetuous and ordered him demoted from his position as general secretary of the USSR. At that moment, Stalin resolved to eliminate his political enemies, beginning with those on the left, and then attacking those on the right. Once rid of his opponents, he took on "the immense task of transforming, in five years, a backward nation into a modern industrial country." As far as Baby M.'s mother and Nurse Vautour were concerned, this was cause for joy. After all, "factories sprouted on the bare plains of Russia, schools were opened, specialists were imported." But the "famous purges" soon convinced them the truth was not so pretty. "One by one, well-known Russian figures appeared before the courts and pleaded guilty to accusations of activities harmful to the state." One by one they were liquidated. The slaughter completed, Stalin and his cohorts settled in comfortably at the head of the state.

෴

Nurse Vautour and the woman who, unbeknownst to her, carried Baby M. in her womb, were in the habit of believing everything the newspapers reported. Their confidence was based on a sort of consensus of knowledge which seemed to them to have always existed. They believed, for example, in the fundamental goodness of Queen Mary, in spite of her expressed predilection for the Duke of Windsor. However, in the case of Stalin, a doubt lingered in their minds. They could not bring themselves to condemn him entirely. The West made a great deal of the Communist threat, constantly reminding everyone that the Reds were trying to infiltrate everywhere and that their singular goal was to impose their diabolical system on the entire world. The two women noted that, on this point, Stalin had behaved rather reasonably from the outset. He wanted to implement revolutionary politics in Russia before going elsewhere (contrary to Trotsky, who would have built socialism simultaneously in several countries). Without knowing it, Baby M.'s mother and Nurse Vautour were taking on the problem of truth, which was also Trotsky's and Stalin's main concern, the former having founded the newspaper *Pravda* (*Truth*) in 1908, and the latter having run it for several years, beginning in 1912.

As for Baby M.'s mother and Nurse Vautour, they had not the slightest interest in the ethics of journalism. They never thought about the relationship between understanding and language. Nevertheless, they were happy to read an article, in *l'Évangéline* of course, entitled "Meaning of Words Changes in Communist Countries," an article published not long after Stalin's death. A Chinese professor exiled in California, who claimed to have experienced the Communist terror in China, drew up a glossary of common expressions which had acquired new meanings under Communist rule. Professor Daniel Hong Lew wrote that, in the

Communist mind, freedom had become "the duty to con-
form to Communist ideas and actions," that the people
comprised "those that supported or were in a position to
support Communism," that democracy implied "consent of
the masses, whether in word or deed," and that peace
was nothing more than "the surrender of non-Communist
forces." As for truth, it consisted of "news and information
which promotes the Communist cause." Professor Hong
Lew also stated that the Reds made systematic use of "the
big lie and brainwashing techniques" to control the people's
ideas. He also offered a description of the "new human
beings that the Reds had vowed to perfect." Essentially,
these were to be "soulless bipeds, human robots whose
individual value was equivalent to the productive value of
horses or cattle." He also spoke of the collective man that
the Communists sought to create. In the Communist view,
"the individual's existence is contingent on his being productive in some manner useful to the Kremlin or if he can
fit like a brick in the wall of a Communist cell, for the
collective man is devoid of personality or nationality." The
article, which originated in Los Angeles, concluded that
the Communist regime tolerated no opposition, and that all
opposition had to be annihilated by "criticism, self-criticism,
and persuasion," all language practices.

ᏬᎾ

In the chapter entitled "Political Modes of Writing" in
Writing Degree Zero, Roland Barthes dwells at some length
on the difference between spoken and written language. He
argues that speech is nothing more than "a mobile series of
approximations" which does not share the "rooted" nature

of writing. He explains that all writing contains "the ambiguity of an object which is both language and coercion [and that] there exists fundamentally in writing a 'circumstance' foreign to language . . . the weight of a gaze conveying an intention which is no longer linguistic," that is, communication. This attenuating "circumstance" "may well express a passion for language, as in literary modes of writing [but] it may also express the threat of retribution, as in political ones: writing is then meant to unite at a single stroke the reality of the acts and the ideality of the ends."

Barthes notes that, "grandiloquent" and "inflated" though it may be, the political writing which characterized the French Revolution only reflected the importance of the real situation. He argues that, if it had not been fulfilled in the "extravagant pose" of revolutionary language, "the Revolution could not have been this mythical event which made History fruitful, along with all future ideas on revolution." Similarly, Marxist revolution also attained final fulfilment in language. However, Barthes insists, Marxist writing shares nothing of the rhetorical amplification of French revolutionary writing. He speaks instead of a "lexicon as specialized and as functional as a technical vocabulary; even metaphors are here severely codified. [And whereas] French revolutionary writing always proclaimed a right founded on bloodshed or moral justification," Marxist writing is presented as "the language of knowledge . . . meant to maintain the cohesion of a Nature."

Barthes feels that, despite having written in a generally pedagogical manner, Marx nevertheless opened the way to the "language expressing value-judgements [which came to] pervade writing completely in the era of triumphant Stalinism." In the Marxist context, each word becomes "a narrow

reference to the set of principles which tacitly underlie it
. . . an algebraical sign representing a whole bracketed set
of previous postulates." Once elevated to the level of a
system, it is "a stability in its explanations and a permanence
in its method" of the Marxist lexicon that actually makes the
so-called permanent revolution possible. Stalin was able to
exploit this system right down to its roots and to engender
a language which transformed the consciousness of his
people. In this coded universe, "*definition*, that is to say
the separation of Good and Evil, becomes the sole content
of all language [. . . and] no longer aims at founding a
Marxist version of the facts . . . but at presenting reality in
a prejudged form." Humanity still has much thinking to do
about the phenomenon of language transforming man while
man transforms language. It concerns the very essence of
reality: always shifting, always in the process of being
defined. This continuum is such that we never know exactly
where to situate the boundary, if such a boundary exists.
The young Stalin, dipping his pen in the inkwell of *Truth*
— that is, of *Pravda* — probably did not imagine that he
would publish, near the end of his life, a theoretical text
entitled *Marxism and Linguistics*. History shows that he was
always acutely conscious of language, for his regime per-
secuted not only men of science, but also philosophers,
linguists, and poets.

తు

Of course, like Nurse Vautour, Baby M.'s mother had not
read *Writing Degree Zero*. And although Professor Hong
Lew's testimony seemed honest enough, it came from too
far away for the two women to get an absolutely true picture

of life behind the iron curtain. The potentially determining testimony came several months later. An Acadian from Lewisville — a Maillet from Bouctouche Bay — had seen the Reds in the flesh: at last, someone who could be believed. A corporal in the American army, he had been wounded by shrapnel from a mortar and held prisoner for twenty-six months by the Communists in Korea. Friends and relatives — Cormiers, Maillets, Goguens, Richards, and Bastaraches — welcomed his return with joyful enthusiasm. *L'Évangéline* was there, as well.

In the article covering the reunion, the reporter noted that the corporal declared himself very happy to be back among his own. And yet, "he only replied after serious reflection, like a man used to watching his words." The ex-prisoner admitted that conditions behind the barbed wire were not as terrible as people had been led to believe. Nevertheless, when he was asked if he had had enough to eat, "our soldier clearly had to fight back a wave of emotions that only those who have shared such an experience could truly understand. He chewed a moment on his lip and answered more or less clearly: 'Some moments were better than others,' and he forced a smile." When asked if the Communists had tried to indoctrinate him, the corporal "looked the reporter in the eye, and weighing his words, confided: 'They tried hard enough,'" which meant that they had tried, and failed.

The reporter, who had not read *Writing Degree Zero* either, had clearly not imagined that he would be up against, in this interview, the superimposition of two systems of understatement: Marxist and Acadian. The remainder of the interview was no more generous in terms of details. Decoding the corporal's laconic answers and waves of emotion provided nothing of substance. In the end, the soldier explained that he could say nothing, that bad press could provoke the Communists and push them to take revenge on the remaining prisoners. The journalist took note, and the atmosphere of the reunion turned cheerful once again. In the spirit of the celebration, he nevertheless risked asking the corporal if he intended to marry during his furlough: "at which point the corporal shook off his emotions and produced a radiant smile nothing short of extraordinary," before replying: " 'I haven't yet made up my mind.' "

In spite of her numerous occupations and concerns (four small children and a fifth on the way), Baby M.'s mother took the time to reread the article. Unfortunately, the second reading provided no further information than she had gleaned from the first. Unsatisfied but feeling guilty for neglecting her housework, she concluded, to speed things along, that the poor soldier had probably not seen much of the Communist world outside his prison camp. Nurse Vautour, who had also read and reread the report, took a more critical stance. She decided to be wary of a man who could produce an extraordinary smile at the mention of marriage, while maintaining the possibility that he might not get his feet wet.

ట

In July 1953, a poll conducted among United Press editors placed Stalin's death and Georgi Malenkov's ascension to the head of the Soviet world at the top of the most-significant-events list for the first half of the year. It was the first time the press agency's editors were polled in the middle of a year, which demonstrates how much busier than usual the semester had been. There followed, in order of importance: President Eisenhower's inauguration in the United States; the negotiation of a cease-fire in Korea; riots in East Germany; the execution of the Rosenbergs; Elizabeth II's coronation; the Tokyo air disaster; tornadoes in the United States; the conquest of Mount Everest; and the nuclear test in Nevada. Also on the list were the McCarthy investigations; a prisoner exchange in Korea; the transformation of Christine Jorgensen; Einstein's unified-field theory; and the Braves' move from Boston to Milwaukee.

Stalin's death maintained its top ranking in the end-of-the-year poll. It was followed by the end of the Korean war and the freeing of prisoners of war; the making of a hydrogen bomb in Russia and Eisenhower's plan for the peaceful use of atomic energy; the return to power of the Republicans in the United States; the Rosenbergs's execution; the capital punishment of little Bobby Greenlease's kidnappers; Elizabeth II's coronation; the repercussions of McCarthyism on Harry Truman; the East German rebellion; and the drought in the American west along with its effect on agricultural prices. Although they did not all make the top ten list of the most important events of the year, most of the events selected in the July poll did receive some votes at the end of the year, except for Christine Jorgensen's transformation and Einstein's unified field theory. In the opinion of the international press of the period, the latter events would not stand the test of time.

But could one believe everything the United Press said? A few days after Stalin's death, the service had issued a dispatch claiming that Stalin had been assassinated and that he was already dead when the Kremlin announced his illness. The dispatch quoted an exclusive report from the *Hartford Current* which was based on letters received by a Russian immigrant living in that Connecticut city. The source insisted on remaining anonymous, fearing reprisals against his parents living in Moscow. According to this "reliable authority on the situation in Russia," the murder of Stalin had been "kept secret because of the reaction it would cause among the Russian people and in the anti-Communist world."

3

The Problem of Knowledge

Banquet for Einstein — Regularity and irregularity of time — A monarchy on the brink of obsolescence — The two-edged sword of reality turns against the Duke of Windsor — Baby M.'s mother and the allegory of the crown — Definitely not a sinecure — The joy of a Connor Thermo washing machine — Journalists battle obscurantism — An honourable profession after all — The Trieste Affair: frontier city at the world's centre — God and the species of novelists — The realm of the unconscious

A SPECIAL BANQUET to celebrate Einstein's seventy-fourth birthday was held in the United States on Saturday, March 14, 1953, that is, in the middle of the twenty-day period that separated the deaths of Stalin and Queen Mary. According to the United Press release published by *l'Évangéline*, Einstein, "who rarely spoke in public," lifted a corner of the veil that covered the origin of his scientific career. He recalled being fascinated by a compass at the age of five. The celebrated physicist with the tousled white hair explained that it was "the trembling needle drawn to the north by a force which he did not understand" that set him on the road to the "most profound mysteries of the universe." He added that plane geometry, which he studied at the age of twelve, also greatly influenced his evolution, but he was careful to point out that "no one knows what causes a particular reaction in an individual," and that, in truth, "man knows very little about what goes on deep within himself."

It did not take the world very long to recognize Einstein's genius: he was awarded the Nobel Prize in physics in 1921, at the age of forty-two. As well as initiating a kind of mutation in science, Einstein's thinking had the primordial consequence of demonstrating that science is not immutable, that humanity must continuously restructure its knowledge according to that which it seeks to know. Einstein's theories also had philosophical ramifications, modifying even the human conception of the universe. The theory of relativity, for example, cast a new light on our notions of time and space. The idea of relativity helped to renew thinking in general by demonstrating that the contextual universe is as important as the universal context. Thus, depending on the context, time might just as easily represent regularity as irregularity, to cite but one example.

❧

If the Duke of Windsor, alias Edward VIII, had hoped that time would heal the wound he had inflicted on his noble family in 1936, he was disappointed, first in 1952, on the occasion of his brother George VI's premature death, again in 1953, with the demise of his mother, Queen Mary, and once more at his niece Elizabeth II's coronation. Back among his family after a fifteen-year exile (during which he never abandoned hope of being recalled to his nation to serve his people), the deposed king discovered, beneath a polite and friendly surface, a hard crust covering nothing but granite. To her dying day, his mother never forgave her eldest and reputed favourite son for having put his personal interests — that is, his love for Mrs. Wallis Simpson — ahead of those of the nation, which had sacrificed so much during the war. So hurt was Queen Mary by Edward VIII's decision that she never consented to meet the woman he loved and without whom he claimed he was not a whole man. The dowager never forgave Mrs. Simpson for having literally robbed England of a most promising king, and forcing the coronation of his badly prepared brother, whose health and temperament were far less suitable to the duties of a monarch. George VI, the brother in a sense condemned to rule, also adopted Queen Mary's coolness towards Edward VIII, who was demoted to the rank of duke. This fraternal contempt lasted until George VI's death, a death about which the royal family did not personally inform the Duke of Windsor. The latter was profoundly humiliated to learn of his brother's death from a mob of New York reporters waiting at the door of his hotel for his comments.

The royal family's enmity had many other unfortunate consequences for the Duke and Duchess of Windsor. Among them, the duke had to wage a struggle to maintain his royal pension. He also ran into a wall of refusal every time he expressed his desire to return to live in England. By 1953, this intransigence had finally convinced him to abandon any demands for a royal title for his beloved Wallis,

but he maintained the hope of attending his niece Elizabeth's coronation with the duchess on his arm. The duke
imagined the coronation as the occasion for a great family
reconciliation before the whole world. It turned out to be
probably his last great disappointment. He was informed
that, according to protocol, he had the right to attend the
ceremony, but without his wife. The real hope was that he
would publicly announce his intention not to attend, thereby sparing the royal family and himself any embarrassment.
The duke had no choice but to accept the situation. He was
granted only one concession: that no other deposed monarch
would attend the ceremony. In the end, he watched the
June 2, 1953, coronation on television, from a Paris salon,
whence he wrote a report commissioned by the United Press.

For years, prior to Elizabeth II's ascension to the throne,
Baby M.'s mother and Nurse Vautour had been following
the ups and downs of the House of Windsor. The royal
family was omnipresent in the lives of the two women,
thanks to the strongly loyalist anglophone majority of their
surroundings. Although their family and close friends were
entirely of Acadian and Catholic stock, there was always a
loose link — be it by blood or mere acquaintance — with
British heritage. If the dignified stance of George V and
his wife Queen Mary had fully justified this interest, the
abdication of their energetic and charming son for the love
of a twice-divorced American had the effect of a knife thrust
deep into the heart of the royal portrait. Because it should
be remembered that, for some time, the entire institution of
the monarchy had been teetering, like some gigantic precious stone, on the verge of obsolescence.

The charming Edward VIII's dramatic and romantic gesture spread like a rent in the Empire and awakened discord

over the issues of duty, honour, and love. Even Winston Churchill exhausted his skills at negotiation and reconciliation. After the initial shock, large numbers of people expressed their sympathy for the lovers. In spirit, Baby M.'s mother and Nurse Vautour took the duke and duchess's side. Which is why they remained, in a sense, obsessed by the image of the duke crying hot tears for his dead mother, Queen Mary. The situation was perplexing: a mother (not to mention a queen full of rectitude) repudiating a son who, like herself, had simply refused to compromise. Because, in fact, there were those who had encouraged the young king to rule while maintaining a secret liaison with Mrs. Simpson. The fact that Edward VIII refused such a compromise really demonstrates that he inherited his mother's rectitude. Yet, as reward for this filial loyalty, he was expelled from the clan. All things considered, it was this judgement-without-appeal which led Baby M.'s mother and Nurse Vautour to conclude that Queen Mary must really and truly have had a preference for this son who later betrayed, in spite of himself, and so profoundly, the impenetrable English esprit de corps.

ഇ

The expression "monarch's duty" is not too strong to describe the task that falls to the heirs of the British crown. Elizabeth II's coronation was the opportunity (for those who had never before thought about it) to realize the seriousness of this reign. *L'Évangéline* did its part to instruct its readers on the rights and duties of British royalty. In so doing, the Acadian newspaper was merely following the lead of a world-wide information campaign, which began in January

1953 with the announcement of the date of the coronation of Elizabeth II, who would have been named Victoria had anyone entertained the slightest possibility that she would one day sit on the throne (a highly unlikely possibility until her uncle abdicated). This information on the rights and duties of the British royalty was disseminated in the midst of a celebratory frenzy, which gradually gained momentum as the time of the ceremony, scheduled for June in Westminster Abbey, grew closer. In spite of strict instructions forbidding any commercial exploitation of the event and its symbols, the frenzy, which was mounting daily, inevitably led to a kind of merchandising mania. There were coronation ties, and hairdos for women "not born to nobility" who were going to attend the ceremony. One could have one's moustache trimmed like those that would be sported by the military, or purchase a photograph of the Benedictine monk who would oversee production of the silk required for the queen's dress. The monk Dom Edmund had allowed himself to be photographed examining one of the numerous webs produced by silk worms fed on mulberry leaves at the Farnborough Abbey. The frenzy was also nourished by a daily emergence of details about the balls, evenings, receptions, and tea and champagne parties that marked the event. Even the province of Quebec declared a holiday. Among other things, every Canadian child born on June 2 would receive a silver spoon from Governor General Vincent Massey, as "a personal gift in solemn memory."

And what solemnity! Reading *l'Évangéline*'s articles on the profound meaning of "this deployment of crowns, sceptres, gold spurs, and priceless dresses," one could not do otherwise but take the ceremony seriously. To begin with, the ritual dated back more than a millennium, whence its

archaic nature, and then there was the unshakeable quality
of the crown: "a symbol dominating differences of religion
or political affiliation." The woman who had been carrying
Baby M. in her womb for more than three months took the
time to read these long articles on the allegory of the crown.
She knew in advance that she would not understand it all,
but she enjoyed abandoning herself to the thrust of knowledge; she compared the experience to the comforting
effects of a good cup of tea. Every day at this hour, she
thanked the heavens for blessing her four children with the
gift of the siesta, and her husband with a "social vocation
in the form of a journalistic calling."

And so it was that Baby M.'s mother learned that the
three-hour ceremony would be divided into five parts:
the Introduction, comprising the Recognition and the Oath;
the Consecration; the receiving of the royal vestments and
insignia resulting in the Coronation; the Installation on the
throne and the Homage; and finally, the celebration of
the Holy Communion. Having vowed to govern the Crown
territories according to their respective laws and customs,
the future sovereign would receive the unction, which alone
allowed her to take up the insignia of royalty and the crown.
During the Consecration, the archbishop officiating would
touch the queen's hand with the sabre of memory as a
reminder "to render justice, halt the progress of iniquity,
protect the Holy Church of God, aid and defend widows
and orphans, restore that which has fallen into ruin, maintain that which has been restored, punish and reform that
which is not in order, and confirm that which is in good
order." After the Coronation, the archbishop would declare:
"God crown you with a crown of glory and right, so that,
possessing a just faith and the fruit of numerous good acts,

you may be granted the crown of an immortal realm by the grace of Him whose kingdom is everlasting." The article being read by Baby M.'s mother went on to explain that, although the mass had been replaced by a "symbolic service" and "priests of a Christian heresy" had replaced the Roman bishops, the ceremony continued to reflect, in large part, the Catholic history of England, which had crowned its last Catholic king, James II, in 1685. In fact, throughout the ceremony, the word *Protestant* would be pronounced but once, whereas the word *Catholic* would be spoken twice: once as the archbishop of Canterbury placed the ring on the fourth finger of the right hand, saying: "Receive the ring of royal dignity and the seal of the Catholic faith." Furthermore, the "Veni Creator," the "Gloria in Excelsis," the "Sanctus" and, following the last blessing, a "solemn and triumphant 'Te Deum'" would be sung. Catholics would also be gratified to witness, immediately after the ceremony, the presentation to the sovereign of a Holy Bible, "the most precious object the world can give."

In a subsequent article, *l'Évangéline* explained that, although the queen "does not rule over us by divine right, nor even by our choice, we participate in her dignity without conferring it on her." And though there exists "no precise information regarding what the queen can do" beyond her three rights within the British constitution (the right to be consulted, the right to offer encouragement, and the right to give warning), the kingdom continues to recognize in her "a source of honour" and "a source of justice." As the ultimate symbols of selflessness, the king and queen are the guardians of that "rare gift of making us feel instinctively their innate goodness," thereby winning the respect and affection of their subjects. Also, "they have all eternity to accomplish their important destinies . . . guided by stars only they can see." As a matter of fact, many of these attributes were in evidence in the photograph of Elizabeth II wearing the royal vestments, the imperial crown, and the purple robes: "in her left hand, she held the globe, emblem of sovereign power, and in the right the sceptre with the cross, symbol of royal power and of justice." On her wrists she wore "the bracelets of sincerity."

ℭ

As one observer put it, the work of a monarch is no sinecure. At the time of Edward VIII's abdication, there were those who suggested that George V's heir had never really wanted to rule, and that his love for Wallis Simpson was nothing more than a pretext to extricate himself from the colossal responsibility. No such rumours ever circulated regarding Elizabeth II, of whom it was said that she appeared to possess all the necessary qualities to fulfil her role. In 1952, immediately following the death of her father, she took the affairs of the realm in hand, so that even before her coronation, her bravery, composure, and courage, as well as her social, democratic, and familial sensibilities, were already generally recognized. People spoke also of her charm and her enviable beauty, which reflected an inner "spiritual and moral beauty," her extraordinary resistance to fatigue, and her profound sense of duty. At the age of twenty-seven — already wife, mother of two children, housekeeper, business woman, and landlord — Elizabeth agreed to take her turn as "one of the pillars of the axis on which the universe turns."

Sitting in her rocking chair in the corner of her kitchen,

her feet up on a stool and a cup of tea in her hand, Baby M.'s mother tries to imagine the life of the new queen, whose age is identical to hers. The brand new washing machine hums beside the sink as it chews on its fourth load of clothes of the day. As they do every day after lunch, the children are sleeping in the next room. Their pregnant mother will lie down too, as soon as this last load is done. This fifth pregnancy is really what finally convinced her to buy — on credit, of course — the Connor Thermo washer. She did not choose this particular brand because it was "the most beautiful washer on the market," as the ads claimed, but rather because it was available at Lounsbury's, where it was more convenient to deliver her monthly payments. The cost of the machine was certainly a problem — she was not in the habit of buying the most expensive brands — but she managed to convince herself that, in this case, her decision was justified.

Though Baby M.'s mother was often obliged to make decisions that affected the lifestyle of the entire household, she never thought of herself in the glorious role of queen of the household. Nor was she conscious of having been selected by some "divine favour" for her role as Catholic mother, at once "nurse, prioress, educator, martyr," and "queen." If she was conscious of anything, it was of the concrete work of a housekeeper, work that the most elementary activities of family life will nullify in the wink of an eye. Nevertheless, Baby M.'s mother did not minimize the importance of her position or her role in the hierarchy. She was perfectly aware that everyone had the same duty: to look after their own. Whether it was Baby M.'s mother's devotion to her household, her husband-the-scriptor's to the Acadian nation, or Queen Elizabeth II's to the Empire, all applied themselves to honour and protect their own. Their tasks had been clearly designated and all dedicated themselves without hesitation; no doubt because each, in their respective domain, realized that nothing was guaranteed, that at any moment life could come apart, and that God himself would not suffice to make it better.

҂

The threat of dissolution came from everywhere. It came in such varied forms that one could never stop learning how to understand and recognize it. Which meant that one had to examine everything twice. The result was a kind of long, slow trial. And such hard work. Who to believe? What to believe? That letter from a reader, for example, denouncing the publication in *l'Évangéline* of "several articles with historical pretensions expounding in servile manner the glories of the [English] nobility." Unable to sit idly by while there "subsists in the midst of the twentieth century an illusion that has cast its malicious shadow over centuries throughout history," the offended reader felt compelled to set the record straight by pointing out that "there is but one true nobility . . . that of the heart [and that] the only difference the Creator made between human beings is that of woman's submission to man." Suddenly, Baby M.'s mother felt a mouthful of tea freeze in her throat.

And what about Julius and Ethel Rosenberg? Treacherous spies or saintly innocents? They had been waiting almost two years to be taken to the electric chair in Sing Sing's death house, while their execution was continually delayed. Even Einstein and Pius XII had called for the commutation of their death sentences. Finally, following reprieve upon reprieve, the Rosenbergs expiated their atomic crime on June 19, under "a blazing sunset." That same day, President Eisenhower had refused their final appeal for clemency, arguing that "the crude design of the first atomic bomb" they traitorously delivered to a Russian agent "could one day cause the death of millions of innocent people." In the preceding months, it had been suggested that the Rosenbergs be offered in exchange for the freedom of American prisoners, including the Associated Press correspondent in Prague, William Oatis. Which only goes to show that journalists did carry some weight, though not enough to have the suggestion adopted. This time, the kick that Baby M. delivered to the uterine wall was felt by her mother, who experienced a gurgling sensation in her womb.

Journalists were, in fact, often victims of the war they waged on ignorance. But though they were blamed for their mistakes and ridiculed for their determination, no one would deny them their role in the development of the twentieth century. UNESCO had consecrated the profession in 1948, in a judgement as clear as day: "henceforth journalism is a profession, and the condition of journalist is considered honourable." Lester B. Pearson — who, in 1953, was Canada's minister of foreign affairs and quietly moving towards the position of secretary general of the UN and the Nobel Peace Prize — also recognized the importance of the profession. He complained, however, that "news reports were so efficient that the results of diplomatic discussions were sometimes made public before they were actually conducted." As for President Eisenhower, he generally fostered a spirit of camaraderie with journalists. He allowed them to call him Ike, publicly declaring that this familiarity in no way diminished his presidential dignity.

Although journalists were widely respected, from time to time it was nice to hear that someone had put one in his place, just so their heads would not swell up too much. The husband of famed soprano Helen Traubel was among those who, in 1953, afforded the non-journalistic masses an opportunity to avenge, if only slightly, the tension caused by the constant presence of the pen, the microphone, and the eye of democracy. When a reporter wanted to know if director Rudolf Bing had put Madame Traubel out of the Metropolitan Opera "for good" because she had been singing in night clubs, her husband called the man an imbecile. Madame Traubel's husband's exasperation in the face of this rather harmless question demonstrates the extent to which the omnipresence of journalists had begun to annoy people. Cardinal Spellman of New York had his own small moment of glory in this respect. Arriving from a three-week tour of Europe, he was obliged to correct reports of his having been ill during his trip on the continent. When he explained that the source of these claims was a reporter who had examined him with a pencil rather than a doctor armed with a stethoscope, everyone understood.

❧

And that's the way it was. No matter what end of the social fabric you took up, you could never be sure you were holding a solid thread of knowledge, whether popular or scientific. Even Pius XII found it necessary to intervene twice during the year. He dealt, first of all, with the excesses and lacunae of psychoanalysis, arguing that this sort of research ought not to "reduce man to the level of a beast,

on the pretext of sounding the depths of his nature." Later
he denounced eugenics, the new "daring science of heredity" that raised the threat of intervention to perfect the race.

Like all good journalists, although more or less un-
schooled in these fields, Baby M.'s father never lost sight of
his role in the chain of knowledge. Everything he reported
would shed some additional light on a world that so
fervently distrusted obscurantism. Thus, between an article
entitled "Yugoslavs Accuse Italians" (the Trieste Affair) and
another entitled "Russians Want to Rest" (after the Stalinist
regime), one learned "What the French Think of Americans," which was that "the Americans are like big babies
who won't mind their own business." This sort of article
made one smile and was easy to read straight through to
the end. One discovered that, despite this flaw, the French
liked the Americans more than they did any other people,
except the Swiss. And even though the average Frenchman
felt the Americans were "hypnotized by their fear of Communism," when it came to welcoming a stranger into his
home, he would choose an American over anyone else. The
article provided other details, among them the fact that
more than half of the eight thousand French people who
had been polled did not like jazz, and that an even greater
majority disapproved of chewing-gum.

The Trieste Affair, however, presented a far greater interpretative challenge. Trieste, the Adriatic port under dispute
between Italy and Yugoslavia, served as a kind of barometer
of the Western world's support for Tito's regime. The
democratic powers, having grown more tolerant towards
the Yugoslav regime since the famous Marshall had distanced himself from Moscow, were hesitant to intervene
militarily in the conflict. In 1947, the Treaty of Paris had

created the Free Territory of Trieste, a neutral territory divided into two zones: one under English and American supervision, the other under Yugoslavian control, with the entire operation under UN authority. In 1953, when Yugoslavia threatened to retake the entire territory which it had occupied in 1945, Italian leaders remained calm but firm in the face of what they judged to be a form of blackmail. Nevertheless, the Italian army made ready to intervene in case Yugoslavia decided to execute its threat. The following year, Italy finally obtained its slice of the pie. The Free Territory of Trieste was divided once and for all between Italy and Yugoslavia, Tito's government having agreed to give up the port zone coveted by the Italians.

Annals of popular knowledge (*l'Évangéline*, the *dictionnaire Robert des noms propres*, a guide to the one hundred most interesting towns and villages of Italy) do not elucidate Yugoslavia's motivation for this compromise. Perhaps the Yugoslavians realized that Trieste had never known prosperity, except under the rule of the Hapsburgs — that is the Austrians — and that neither the Yugoslavians nor the Italians would reverse this historical determinism. Or maybe, already conscious of its inability to halt the port's decline, Yugoslavia had simply agreed to abandon Trieste to its destiny as a frontier city inclined, like so many others, to do as it pleases, come what may. If such an intuition did exist, it turned out to be pretty good, for even under Italy's wing, Trieste continues to boast an identity entirely its own. The hour's distance from Venice preserves Trieste from the international tourist traffic which floods Italy, and allows the few hundred thousand Triestans to live at a slower pace than the other city-dwellers of Italy. Their tourists are Yugoslavians who come across the border to buy the latest fashions in shoes and clothing. In addition to the merchants, many Triestans make an honourable living importing coffee for the roasters and espresso counters throughout the rest of Italy. Others specialize in writing insurance policies for distant clients. Today, thanks to its excellent university and its international institute of theoretical physics, Trieste aspires to a reputation as an international centre for scientific research.

℘

It is also popular knowledge that the journalist's trade is based on reality — that is to say on verifiable and verified facts. Those claiming to be journalists cannot simply say whatever comes into their heads; they must report what is. They can be more or less astute, but they must absolutely avoid distorting the facts to promote one point of view over another. Writing novels offers more latitude to someone who has difficulty sticking to the facts. Novelists not only have the right to fabulate, it is their duty. One can like or dislike, agree or disagree with a novelist's point of view, but there is no denying his or her voyage into the imaginary. To do so would be, in Pius XII's words, to "reduce man to the level of a beast," to shackle what he called "the secrets of his nature."

Nevertheless, in order to write, the novelist requires the raw material that is reality. He needs reality — and the language which is part of reality — to break through the wall that would enclose him, a wall that strangely resembles the wall of knowledge. In that sense, the novelist employs reality as a weapon in his assault on the wall. Described this way, writing a novel can seem quite dangerous. And it is, because there is always the danger that the novelist's weapon, somehow or other, will turn against him. He is never safe from the reality — from the word — that wounds. Nor does the novel have the power to eradicate this wound, just as it does not have the power to eradicate reality. It can only hope to make it flower. If God deserves any praise, the fact of having tossed a handful of novelists into the universe surely has something to do with it. Thanks to this gesture, every event reported by a journalist for the greater good of democracy is doubled by an aura. The source of this aura is the possibility that the event will be taken up and rewritten by a novelist, for the greater good of humanity. Thus, fabulous Trieste, having drunk from many fountains, settled on coffee, theoretical physics, and insurance policies, and produced a cuisine which combined its Viennese, Italian, Hungarian, and Balkan heritages.

ↄ

Baby M.'s mother and Nurse Vautour did not follow the Trieste Affair closely. *L'Évangéline* often spoke of the precarious situation in that corner of Europe, but the crux of the problem continued to resist understanding. It was another of those political situations which are difficult to grasp from a distance. And so, in July 1954, when the newspaper announced that an Italian division would soon take control of the zone the Yugoslavian adversary had finally agreed to give up, Baby M.'s mother and Nurse Vautour sensed there was reason to rejoice. They had no time to explore the issue further, however, being too busy that day with Baby M.'s hospitalization. And yet, there was, in the mother's gesture of placing Baby M. into the arms of

Nurse Vautour, something akin to Yugoslavia's turning over the port of Trieste to Italy. The mother, like Yugoslavia, experienced the contradictory feelings of her surrender: on the one hand, the weight of failure, on the other, the relief that comes to those who can recognize defeat and act accordingly. For her part, Nurse Vautour, like Italy, accepted Baby M. with all the assurance of the medical world (that is, the Western world), but knew that no effort must be spared to put Baby M. (that is, Trieste) on the road to a healthy development.

In Baby M.'s case, medical science accomplished its duty. Without really understanding the cause of her illness, and without really being able to stop its progress, medical science sustained the child through her time of crisis, ensuring that the tiny body took in a sufficient amount of nutrients in spite of its difficulty absorbing them. In short, medical science kept Baby M. alive. And yet, during her hospitalization in July 1954, before regaining her health, Baby M. sank to the lowest point of her illness. The attending physician was not sure he could save the child. Despite her unshakeable strength of character, Nurse Vautour also feared that Baby M. might be swept away by her own turmoil. For, deep down, Nurse Vautour felt Baby M. was too capricious for her own good. And though she granted Baby M.'s right to enter life through the door of her choosing, she begged her, for heaven's sake, to stay clear of the door of malabsorption. Which only shows to what extent Nurse Vautour was ignorant of the measures taken by the Almighty to ensure the reproduction of the species of novelists. In this particular case, the seed of writing was buried deep in Baby M.'s entrails, which may be true for all writers, given their tendency to navel-gaze.

And yet, as she moves from her mother's arms to those of Nurse Vautour, Baby M. has no idea what is happening. Like Trieste's, the secret of her survival lies in a distant past, in a sense of time and the passage of time that humanity, in its rush to live, struggles daily to forget. For Baby M., nothing changes. Life is nothing but the womb of her intestinal struggles, which require all her energy and which, in devouring her, maintain her link to life. Because Baby M.'s spirit is already in transit. It can know nothing, because it is already gone. It is elsewhere, in exile, in the realm of the unconscious.

4

A Writing Scenario

To believe or not to believe in God — The mad undertaking of the novel — Far from futile — The slightly horrible effect of rising water — The infinite diffusiveness of life — A sensation of absence — The baseball base as a resting place — The seriousness of the comic and the truth of falsehood — The present as a possibility — Baldness and transsexuality — Denial and the progress of science — Mysteries and contours of civilizations — The ultimate shape of things — The quest for a centre — Mussolini's tomb and the miracle of the Virgin's tears

NOT ALL NOVELISTS believe in God, and many of those who believe in Him only do so sporadically. This is a shame, because there are few other ways to maintain your serenity while writing an out-of-control novel. In their longing for a kind of logic, novelists tend to panic when what they are trying to say doesn't really seem to fit into the story. At such times, they may conclude they have failed in their task, allowed themselves to get side-tracked, or simply not worked hard enough. Because novelists often have the impression that they are in control of the writing of their novels. Poor things. Rather than limiting themselves to lending intelligence and intuition to that which wants to be expressed, novelists who try too hard to control what emerges from their pens risk drowning in their own ink. They would do better to let themselves float above all logical considerations and calculations, and drift with the current. Even at the risk of running aground or taking a wrong turn. God will easily forgive them their sins of illogic, He Himself being constantly accused of committing them.

The novelist also tends to lose himself in the relationship between his story and History. In fact, he is never entirely sure on what plane he is telling (his)tory. Just as in films, a troubling soft focus always forms around the thing that needs to be shown with precision. On the other hand, a telephoto lens deprives the novelist of any depth of vision, crushing all relief, flattening the very vision which was responsible for pulling him out of his lethargy in the first place and dragging him to his work desk. This difficulty caused by the story, or History, probably explains why every novelist engaged in the writing process swears this book will be his or her last. Obviously no one in his or her right mind would ever willingly get on this merry-go-round again. History, which in the beginning draws us like a majestic statue, turns out to be, from the inside, a damp and cavernous enclave, complete with bats flying about and stalactites dripping into a still and almost certainly bottomless lake, across which we are nevertheless called to venture. A nightmare! To the point where one might well wonder: why take up this occupation? And this is precisely where fiction begins.

The ball returns. Each ball is a challenge.

ↄ

Élizabeth and Brigitte are sitting face to face in Brigitte's office, a high-rise office reeking of success, complete with leather sofa, art objects, etc., etc. The windows the size of movie screens are at the perfect distance from the ground, not too high to make out the comings and goings of humanity, yet high enough to keep one's distance from the futility of these comings and goings. From this height, the world does not seem ugly and life is not such an impasse. Naturally, from this height, any downtown looks good, even Montréal's. To Brigitte, the spectacle of the mildly exciting city remains the same, day after day. There is nothing to wait for. Élizabeth, on the other hand, when she looks down at the hustle and bustle, can't help but feel as though she were on the verge of a celebration. The sight of this feverishness is especially useful at this moment. Sitting silently, the two women have drifted each into her own thoughts. To tell the truth, it was Élizabeth who'd been doing most of the talking. Now her silence seems relatively natural. Whereas Brigitte's, as she was mostly listening, is rather compromising.

And the ball returns.

The time that elapses between two swings of the racquet represents, in Brigitte's mind, a perfect time period. Were she called upon to invent a unit of time, that would be it. Her entire life passes as though it were superimposed on this rhythm. Brigitte can feel this cadence in every important or happy moment, and sometimes, she imposes this rhythm on situations herself. But Brigitte has, of course, never externalized her consciousness of this rhythm. And people in her presence never suspect they are playing a tennis match.

Each ball is a challenge.

Brigitte can do nothing to beat back the silence, whose grip on her only grows stronger, even though it appears compromising. In fact, she is a little surprised to find herself plunged into a state that seems to want to expand and take over. She searches for an idea, a word that might end the invasion. All she sees is the image of water slowly rising, above her feet first, then her ankles, calves, knees, thighs. Nor is this tidewater, from which one easily escapes by taking a few steps back. It's more like water coming up from a basement, filling up one floor after another, water coming from below, from which escape is impossible. But there's something slightly horrible in this description, which really has nothing to do with what Brigitte is feeling.

Brigitte knows very well that this thing she is feeling cannot be directly ascribed to Élizabeth's presence in her office. She knows that Élizabeth is only a thread, a concrete symbol of the moment. Her friend asks nothing from her other than a moment of friendship like so many they have shared in the past. And since Brigitte has always had a fundamental disposition towards friendship for Élizabeth, she does not see what the problem could be today. All the same, Brigitte doesn't know what is going on. She has difficulty distinguishing between what comes from within and what comes from without. It is as though she were subjugated by the infinite diffusiveness of life.

The ball returns. Each ball is a challenge.

For her part, Élizabeth has allowed herself to become somewhat numbed by the calm of the office and the soft lighting. As though she had suddenly been transported to an oasis of tranquillity. Brigitte's silence does not surprise her. She knows there is nothing to say, at least for the time being. But she knows something else as well. She knows she has reached a kind of end, a sort of degree zero. The same is true for Brigitte, although Brigitte does not think in those terms. This moment that resembles nothing she has ever known does not frighten Élizabeth in the least. All the same, a strange image forms in her mind. She imagines herself shoving her fingers into her sternum, tearing open her ribcage, and thrusting her lungs and heart out into the open. She imagines holding her heart in her hands, in the open air. She sees and feels it beating. Then she lifts her lungs, feels them inflating and deflating against her palm. She likes the warmth and autonomy of these organs, as well as the oily blood that covers her hands and forearms. But there's something slightly macabre in this description which really has nothing to do with what Élizabeth is feeling.

Élizabeth often gets a feeling of emptiness in her chest, as though there were nothing inside her ribcage. Nor in her breasts. All this part of her body reminds her of the shape of a missing piece to a puzzle. The absence ends at her stomach, which she can feel quite clearly, along with her sex and her legs. She can also feel her shoulders, arms, neck, and head. She feels her back too. But she feels nothing in her chest. There are moments, when someone is caressing her body, that she does feel something. Or, at least, she forgets the emptiness in her chest. Even if that person is only touching her hand. Perhaps she is feeling, through this touch, the heart, lungs, and full chest of the other person.

e/s

So, two women, now face to face, now side by side. Brigitte and Élizabeth. Élizabeth and Brigitte. We would have to remain a long time in their presence, in this room, to gain some small sense of the distance they have travelled. Though they have not attempted to escape it, one might say that their past has caught up with them. Each one knows, though confusedly, that she has arrived at a destination, but not a goal such as we sometimes set for ourselves in our lives. This is rather a kind of rest stop, more or less necessary, more or less desired, not entirely unwelcome to each of them. A little like in baseball, when the home-run-hitter, knowing he can't be put out, takes the time to sink his foot into each base in passing.

In 1953, Brigitte was five years old, an age when everything can be interesting. Her father, a geographer, would talk to her for hours about the contours of the earth, often digressing into the contours of life. It was a game they both played without constraints, without really differentiating between serious talk and fun, or between truth and falsehood. Not to confuse the child, the geographer had found a way to respect reality without making it too complicated, and to reassure her father, the little girl would sometimes pretend she did not understand something. Gradually this universe of explorers and distant lands was augmented by scientific discovery, so that the global geography lesson soon became a study in human aspirations. It was in this universe of determination and great exploits that Brigitte learned about the sound barrier and the two Jacquelines (the air pilots Jacqueline Auriol and Jacqueline Cochrane). She also followed the exploits of the swimmer Florence Chadwick, as she crossed the wild Dardanelles, the Channel with its schools of jellyfish, the straits of Catalina, Gibraltar, and the Bosphorus, and discovered the depths of the ocean and the upper regions of the atmosphere along with the scientist Picard. The eighty-plus days of fasting by the German Willie Schmitz and the Indian Rei Kan were, for their part, instructive as to the possibilities of living without food.

The further geographer and girl advanced in their discovery of the world, the fewer limitations they placed on ways to approach it. Sometimes the game took on enormous proportions. To the delight of the neighbourhood children, father and child staged Ann Davison's feat: her conquest of the Atlantic to avenge her husband's death. The father played the part of Davison the husband, who drowned while he and his wife were attempting to cross the ocean in a three-metre sailing boat. Brigitte then carried the play herself, confidently assuming the role of the thirty-eight-year-old widow who attempted the same crossing alone to honour her husband's memory. In spite of her young age, Brigitte could easily imagine the elasticity of time spent alone on the sea. She imagined it as a déja vu that goes on and on, each fraction of a second opening up into more fractions of a second, as in an implosion. Melting into the rhythm of the waves, she retreated so completely into herself that her young audience was spellbound, unsure whether the heroine was on the verge of losing consciousness or of attaining a higher consciousness.

Father and daughter also followed with great interest the conquest of Everest, focusing especially on Tensing Norkay, Edmund Hillary's Indo-Nepalese companion in the climb.

The presence of a tiny cute dog in the Norkay family portrait (a wife and two daughters) had much to do with this preference. As for Hillary, the two armchair adventurers noted only that he had undertaken the ascent in celebration of Elizabeth II's coronation. Brigitte and her father also knew that some women porters had participated in the expedition, but they did not know if they had reached the peak. As the neighbourhood children continued to demand new scenarios, daughter and father concocted a kind of alpine mutiny by these women porters. The conflict resolved, the leader of the expedition was obliged to admit that the climb would have failed without the endurance of the women.

~

Élizabeth was only one year old in 1953. Her destiny was therefore radically different from Brigitte's and Baby M.'s. Too young or too old, she remained oblivious to the wonders of 1953. All her life, she has felt trapped in this in-between, on the edge of the present. Today, this condition seems clearer to her than ever. Baptized with the name of an as-yet-uncrowned queen, a queen, furthermore, who would have been given another name if the crown had been more clearly destined for her, Élizabeth suspects she may go through her entire life as someone to whom something is either always on the verge of happening, or perhaps was never meant to happen at all.

Élizabeth has just spent almost three days in her car watching the apartment building where she and Claude often met. The latter is a masseur, which was the reason for Élizabeth's visits. This time Élizabeth stayed in her car because she did not want to talk to Claude. She only wanted to know where he was. She now knows that he no longer lives in the building. The terse caretaker finally revealed that the tenant in question had been gone for three months, without leaving a forwarding address. This explains why Élizabeth was unable to reach Claude by phone. At first, there had been an answering machine, then a recorded message stating the number was no longer in service. Although she did not expect much from this man, Élizabeth felt sufficiently hopeful to come and check if he still lived in the place where she had met him.

Whenever she comes to Montréal, Élizabeth always sets aside some time to see her friend Brigitte. The two women met in medical school and have continued to see each other ever since. At this moment, in Brigitte's office, Élizabeth remembers it was Brigitte who introduced her to Claude. Élizabeth would never have made an appointment with a masseur on her own. In fact, the very idea repelled her, but Brigitte's irresistible charms had finally carried the day. And Claude had won her trust. He was discreet but attentive, seductive without trying to be. But, as he spoke little and maintained his distance, Élizabeth concluded this was going to remain a service relationship, so to speak. One day, Brigitte and Élizabeth ran into Claude in town, at an antique shop on Saint-Laurent. It was a Saturday afternoon; Élizabeth remembers it well. Thanks to Brigitte's friendly personality, the three of them chatted for a while. To Élizabeth, Claude seemed relaxed. But this out-of-context meeting had changed nothing, either in the relationship which had been established between their bodies or in Élizabeth's feeling that she could expect nothing more.

❧

Whenever the opportunity presents itself, Brigitte likes to say she has made a career in *the pharmacology of denial.* Having completed her studies in medicine, and after practising for several years in a private clinic, she was recruited by the multinational pharmaceutical where she has now worked for a dozen years. She feels at home in this medical discipline which is concerned with remedies and other forms of reprieve. In the beginning — and this took several years — Brigitte worked hard to acquire a clear understanding of the gargantuan company's operation. She read mountains of documents dealing with everything from scientific research to philosophy and ethics. Thanks to her ability to assimilate a multitude of new ideas and to handle newly acquired knowledge, she was quickly promoted to management ranks. For several years now, she has been planning and supervising the work of a half-dozen research teams.

Brigitte tends to forget the degree of determination with which she has pursued her career. It seemed perfectly natural to want to understand the ins and outs of the company. For several years, she had virtually no social life and did not miss it. She criss-crossed three continents and met a great number of researchers in laboratories across the globe. These meetings were all interesting. And although it was more than she had ever hoped for, and she sometimes felt she was dreaming, she never bragged. She preferred discretion. Only when one steps into her office does Brigitte's enviable status in the working world become obvious.

The spacious and comfortable office reflects a mind as large as it is open, and yet, the office is anything but intimidating. The severity of the classical woodwork and scholarly bookcases is somewhat attenuated by a number of often-surprising eccentric objects. For example, next to the desk there is the life-size sculpture of a witch carrying a crystal ball in one hand and a Bohemian glass bowl filled with tiny packages of Chiclets chewing-gum in the other. Equally impressive, on a pedestal at the rear of the room: the triple- or quadruple-life-size bronze of a human heart sliced in two. But it is in the broken tennis racket, bent almost in two, lying at the foot of a collection of luxuriously bound books, that Élizabeth, with a half smile, recognizes her friend Brigitte: a cool-headed woman, whose rare but inescapable explosions often have a beneficial effect on those around her, probably because they immediately re-establish, for everyone, the fact that there are limits.

Brigitte has only recently adopted the expression *pharma-cology of denial* to describe the orientation of the research teams under her supervision. In the case of the group searching for a chemical solution to the problem of the rejection of transplanted organs, Brigitte realizes that the term *pharmacology of acceptance* would be more appropriate than *pharmacology of denial.* But since she has had to defend some research in the area of transsexualization, she is convinced that denial more than acceptance is what motivates medical research. The object was to create a new hormonal program for sexual transformation. At first, the heads of the multinational were hesitant to undertake such research. They had serious doubts about the profitability of these new drugs. Of course, Brigitte suspected that these gentlemen found the idea of transsexuality rather perverse. She therefore shifted attention onto a derivative area of research emerging from the main hormonal research: a derivative area which held out the promise of a cure for baldness. The gentlemen, who had initially been so reticent, quickly changed their minds and approved all the necessary funds. When Brigitte uses the expression *pharmacology of denial*, she sees the softened faces of these men, all haunted, up to a point, by the image of a bald head.

⁂

On this visit, Élizabeth cannot spend much time with her Montréal friend. She'll be happy just to catch Brigitte in her office before heading back to Moncton. She has nothing in particular to tell her. She would enjoy simply being in her company for a moment, the way one enjoys returning to a familiar place, with all its landmarks and minor changes. Otherwise, she is ready to take up her own life again, with all that is inalterable and fluid about it, and alien too. But this alienation is not a product of her life in Moncton, among Acadians. Rather, it stems from the unexpected way everything happens. Independently of her, independently of her understanding or aspirations. As though life did not come from within, from within her.

Suddenly Élizabeth has arrived at that exact point of existence where the flow of events seems to take precedence over their content, their meaning. She does not really know how to break this thread. Even death no longer seems a sure way out. People die, but life itself continues. Anyway, Élizabeth has no wish to escape from the uninterrupted progress of life. She would simply like to understand its mechanism better, in order to occasionally act on its mystery. In spite of everything, she is often content to remain on the sidelines of life. She's even developed a kind of talent for stepping back, for distancing herself. This allows her to see the big picture of life, somewhat the way humans admire, centuries later, the contours of some ancient civilization. She thinks of her knack for stepping back as treading water: not churning the water in order to swim, but moving just enough to stay afloat. She realizes this way of life is as much an art as a trial.

But Élizabeth also knows that, by treading water all her life, she might never know whether she is in a pool as opposed to a lake, for example, or in a lake as opposed to a sea, or in a sea as opposed to an ocean, or in an unfathomably large body of water. This impossibility of knowing the ultimate size of things will always be a puzzle to Élizabeth. Which explains, in part, her relatively calm nature. Her feeling of living on the edge of the world also has something to do with it. Because sooner or later, the question of the centre arises; sooner or later the question of the centre poses itself. Her silence is all the more profound at this moment, since she realized for the first time a few moments ago, while pushing the button for the elevator, that what exists is probably not a centre of the world, but only the search for such a centre.

ↇↄ

In 1953, Nurse Vautour already had the premonition that everyone was free to locate the centre of the world where he or she wished. She herself had, in a sense, selected Italy. For her, nothing could compare with the dramatic flare of the Italians, certainly not those rose-coloured novels, which had become red-coloured novels in Communist Germany (novels in which the protagonist, "his eyes shining like the rivets of his machine, felt his heart beating like the chairman's gavel in a workers' meeting"), and even less, the transformation, in China, of the iron curtain into a "bamboo curtain." As for South America, nothing seemed to be going on there, aside from the column entitled "In Chile with the Oblate Fathers," which *l'Évangéline* stubbornly maintained, and which Nurse Vautour simply could not bear to read.

Among the events of 1953 which rekindled Nurse Vautour's favourable predisposition towards Italy (her mother used to call it *the Italies*), was the United States' nomination there of their first woman ambassador, the writer Claire Booth Luce, wife of the editor Henry R. Luce. Reports were that Mrs. Booth Luce had made a favourable impression in a country where "women have failed to make a place for themselves in public life." And yet, it seemed to Nurse Vautour that Italian women were doing their share to make a place for themselves. A female member of the national assembly had gone so far as to participate in a brawl on the floor of the parliament. *L'Évangéline* pointed out that she was the first woman to be knocked down onto that floor. On the other hand, the best punch had been thrown at a neo-fascist member, the same man who had stolen the body of Mussolini from the cemetery in Milan, in 1946.

Coincidentally, a few months before the famous brawl, *l'Évangéline* reported that Mussolini's remains had finally been "removed from their secret tomb and buried in the family plot in the north of Italy." The body of *Il Duce* had been kept in a secret place since the famous bodynapping of 1946, which made the tomb "one of Italy's best guarded secrets." Although it seemed clear that Benito Mussolini had rejoined the other members of his family buried in the cemetery at Paderno, near their home village of Predappio, in northern Italy, the government claimed not to know anything about it. This strange silence was augmented by the fact that the story originally filed in Rome was, for the most part, based on rumours. There was confusion also around the exact location of the grave: the article referred both to a family plot out in the open and to a tomb without inscription inside a chapel. Nurse Vautour did not mind these ambiguities so typical of Italian excess and their propensity for exaggeration. She was merely relieved that, having been repatriated to the village of his birth, Mussolini's body had escaped the torrential rains of the last few days, which were sweeping the country from the Apennines to the southern tip of the boot. As for Italy, such a vertical country, Nurse Vautour could hardly imagine it under water. She nevertheless wondered if the flooding threatened the oratory of the Virgin of Sorrows at Syracuse. She did not know that Sicily was separated from the Italian mainland by the Strait of Messina. Nurse Vautour would not have wanted a mere rush of water to annihilate that presumed miracle. She much preferred to imagine the police on alert, calling for reinforcements to control the crowds of pilgrims come to view the terracotta statuette, "one of thousands of such pieces produced by the factories of central Italy."

As a matter of fact, in this particular case, the Church had wasted no time in initiating the process for recognizing a miracle. Such vigilance did not influence Nurse Vautour's opinion of the tears which were purported to have flowed from the statuette, but it did serve to set the scene of a miracle, which contained all the elements to maintain the nurse's interest. The miracle, which consisted in the curing of "desperately ill" people, had begun after the statuette was suspended "above the bed of a Sicilian Communist's pregnant wife." The woman reported feeling "drops falling on her forehead one night when she was in bed; looking up, she saw tears running down the hand-painted clay cheeks of the Virgin. The crying continued for four days, from August 29 to September 1. Pilgrims and the sick came in great numbers as the news spread. The figure was placed in a temporary niche under the house of the woman in question and was later moved into a larger niche in the main square of the town." During the following weeks, "great numbers of sworn testimonies were scrutinized in meetings in Rome and Palermo, the capital of Sicily." At last, in mid-December, "following a final meeting of the Sicilian bishops . . . the archbishop of Palermo announced the Church had recognized the 'supernatural' character of the tears," chemical tests having demonstrated that "the tears were real." One interesting point: the Sicilian Communist's wife gave birth to the child Mariano Natale on the following Christmas day.

i, as in Italy, or the paradoxical sleep.

5

Idle Talk and Composition I

The foundations of a novel — Wave of kidnappings, coffins in tow and fatal fog — A nine-hundred-year-old quarrel — Multiple births and the Melansons's wager — Shortage of nurses and death of a nurse — Journalists and the Nobel Prize — Eroticism sublimated by invention — French custom regarding team of horses — Norwegian custom regarding the Nobel Peace Prize — Double-action Acadia baking powder — Cardinal Feltin and fence posts — Corpuscular theory of light and other metabolisms — Acadians and Fernandel's accent — No small regard for literature — Unending risk of the body

I T   W O U L D   B E   D I F F I C U L T to ascertain exactly how the months, weeks, days, even hours preceding Baby M.'s birth affected the child's psychological makeup. To do so would be to identify a kind of primary impulse, whereas life is quite content to move along in a continuity that elicits no more than a yawn. Only a novelist, whose madness we forgive more readily, would venture into this uncharted territory. And madness is almost a prerequisite for anyone taking on what is essentially a peristaltic enterprise of assimilation and transformation, in which one must experience all the various states of matter in the name of something larger, which lives. For novelists do not live; they grind. They take life apart, revelling in the sight of its countless components, and then spend sleepless nights trying to figure out how to breathe life back into this inert matter. And even if they succeed in putting it all together, they continue to fret over whether the machine will be of any use. Which is to say that, yes, novelists do worry about their contribution to humanity. Although they may not be alone in worrying thus, at least they are always the first to do so. Herein lies the novelist's main privilege, considering his relative powerlessness to change the course of (his)tory. In this regard, intuition and perseverance are more useful than an overly rational approach. For novelists are archaeologists. They may well have an idea of what they are searching for, but they can never predict what they will find. Nothing is guaranteed. All those who wander on this uncertain ground know how slippery the terrain is. This book, for example, which begins with the birth of Baby M. in 1953 and Élizabeth's presence today in her friend Brigitte's Montréal office.

The least we can say about Baby M.'s birth is that, from a strictly environmental point of view, the context was far from reassuring. Two days before the amniotic sac broke, *l'Évangéline* reported a wave of child kidnappings in the United States, a wave that, it was feared, would soon spread to Canada. The following day, the paper offered a story on the sad fate of other children who, during the past year, had died after accidentally locking themselves inside abandoned refrigerators. These tragic deaths had triggered a refrigerator conservation movement of sorts, launched in the hope of inciting people not to discard what were potentially children's coffins. Adding to this rather gloomy atmosphere, a greyish-yellow mist had descended on all of England the very day of Baby M.'s birth. The fog threatened to become deadly in the capital since, although many Londoners had bought protective masks, few were willing to wear them in public. It also turns out that the same day, the Russians opened Stalin's tomb for the first time since his death. The thousands of so-honoured civil servants and workers filing past the preserved remains recognized "the Stalin of yesteryear, though he looked much younger than a man of seventy-three years." In spite of "the hot and stagnant air" in the crypt, the rejuvenating breeze blew clear across to Europe. The day after Baby M.'s birth, *l'Évangéline* announced that England and France had put an end to their nine-hundred-year-old quarrel over the Minquiers Islands, two tiny islands in the English Channel, rich in lobsters and oysters.

℀

Three other babies, three boys — a Cormier, a LeBlanc, and a Thibodeau — were born the same day as Baby M. in Moncton's Hôtel-Dieu l'Assomption. Four babies — three girls and a boy — had also come into the world in Moncton hospitals the day of the coronation: two in Moncton City Hospital and two in Hôtel-Dieu. These last four babies received silver spoons commemorating Elizabeth II's ascension to the throne. The eight newborns were among 417,884 births registered in Canada in 1953, to the delight of the baby-food industry, whose continued prosperity was assured. Other Acadian births also attracted attention in 1953. A couple named Melanson, originally from Bathurst but living in Santa Monica, California, won an unusual wager with the renowned insurance company Lloyd's of London. According to *l'Évangéline*, shortly after learning that his wife was pregnant, Grégoire Melanson bet Lloyd's that his wife would give birth to more than one child. The insurance policy against multiple births cost Mr. Melanson two hundred dollars, but required Lloyd's to pay five thousand dollars per child born after the first. As *l'Évangéline*'s caption beneath the photo of the triplets in the arms of Californian nurse Mary Leopardi put it, the two girls and one boy were worth their weight in gold.

In Canada, this crop of infants, each one as loveable as the next, did nothing to relieve the pressure on hospitals, which were facing a shortage in nurses. According to the president of the Canadian Medical Association, Dr. Charles Burns, the fault lay with doctors, airlines, and military hospitals: doctors because they hired nurses to do office work, airlines because they recruited nurses to work as hostesses, and military hospitals because they did not pay their share of the cost of training nurses. The Hôtel-Dieu l'Assomption was not exempt from this problem. In August 1953, the hospital put out a call to nursing graduates and auxiliaries who had taken extended leave to do their part for "suffering humanity." It was understood that those who responded to the call would be justly rewarded, because it was not money that was in short supply, but rather qualified nurses. In this context, the death of a nurse did not go unnoticed. And all the more so when the nurse in question was a pillar like Florence Breau, long-time director of nurses in Moncton City Hospital. The staff of the hospital had only just moved into a new building to which, sad to say, Nurse Breau was the first patient admitted. Announcing the demise of Miss Breau, hospital administrator Dr. Porter declared that "no successor, regardless of her abilities or goodness, would ever erase the memory of Miss Breau, for those who had had the privilege to work with her or under her orders." Florence Breau had studied in Moncton's Aberdeen High School and in the Villa Maria convent in Montréal. She had completed her training in the nursing school of the very same hospital that had so appreciated her services.

ℰℐ

Journalists are not infallible. While Lester B. Pearson was critical of their talent for anticipation, others deplored their lack of accuracy. Such journalistic weaknesses also existed at *l'Évangéline*, of course. For example, it may be that the Melanson triplets actually earned their parents five thousand rather than ten thousand dollars. Two articles contradicted each other on this question. All the same, such journalistic errors occasionally resulted in happy events in the world. The creation of the Nobel Prizes for example. When Ludwig Nobel, brother of the famous Swedish industrialist and chemist Alfred Nobel, died in Cannes, in 1888, a Parisian newspaper, believing it was Alfred Nobel who had expired, published the headline "Merchant of Death Dies." Although he had made his fortune in explosives and weapons (he perfected dynamite, and a plastic dynamite safer to handle than pure nitroglycerine), Alfred Nobel, who was above all an inventor, was no doubt shaken by the headline, which betrayed the manner in which he would be remembered. Because he had done far more than perfect explosives. Wilhelm Odelberg, historian and Swedish scientist, tells us that Nobel owned no less than 355 patents on inventions in various countries, notably for artificial silk and leather, and for gutta-percha, an electrical insulator. He also maintained a lengthy correspondence with the Austrian novelist Bertha von Suttner, an ardent pacifist. As a result, one year before his death, Alfred Nobel wrote the famous will which so stunned his relations, colleagues, and the Swedish public in general. In leaving his entire fortune to those whose genius would best serve humanity, Alfred Nobel authored his last invention.

Five years passed between the reading of Alfred Nobel's will and the awarding of the first Nobel Prizes, in 1901. It took that long to establish a structure to award the prizes and administer the fortune, because Alfred Nobel had spoken of his intentions to no one. He had even written his will himself, in order not to have to deal with lawyers and risk being disappointed by them once again. It should be said that, at the end of his life, Alfred Nobel was more interested in the phonograph, the telephone, and various types of projectiles than the administrative side of the institution he had created. In other words, the man — a bachelor who shunned high society and lived a very simple life, considering his means — remained extremely inventive to the end. He is not known to have had any love-life to speak of, which leads one to believe that even his emotional life was subordinated to his inventions. For Alfred Nobel, although he was not a novelist, a day without a new idea was a day gone to waste. He was tireless, mastered five languages, and in politics, tended towards social-democracy.

Born in Stockholm in 1833, he grew up in St. Petersburg, Russia, and lived a good part of his life in Paris. He died in Italy, in San Remo, in 1896. As a matter of fact, his long stay in France caused a problem at the time of his succession, as the French state insisted that Mr. Nobel's fortune was legally located in France. The issue was resolved when it was clearly established that Alfred Nobel had transferred to his native Sweden his team of Russian Orloff horses, a gift from his brother Ludwig. (The three Nobel brothers, known as the "European Rockefellers," had become rich primarily by operating oil wells in Baku, on the Caspian Sea.) And according to French custom, a man's wealth was inventoried on the property where he kept his team of horses.

As brief as his testament was, Alfred Nobel's intentions were clear: each year to reward someone who had made an important discovery or invention in physics, in chemistry, and in medicine and physiology. A fourth prize was to be awarded to an author of a literary work of an "idealist nature," and a fifth prize would crown the efforts of someone who had done the most to foster good relations among nations, to abolish or reduce arms, and to bring people together around the theme of peace. (The prize for political economy was created in the memory of Alfred Nobel by the Swedish Riksbank in 1968, to mark its tercentenary.) The great inventor's will stipulated that the Swedish Academy of Sciences would award the physics and chemistry prizes, the Karolinska Institute of Stockholm the one for medicine or physiology, and the Swedish Academy of Letters the literary prize. The Nobel Peace Prize was to be awarded by the Norwegian parliament, the Storting. Sweden and Norway were politically united at the time Alfred Nobel wrote his will, but when the union was dissolved in 1905, the Storting maintained the role Mr. Nobel had assigned to it.

❧

Like Scandinavia in Alfred Nobel's time, the Moncton area and Acadia in general offered little to attract the attention of the world during the first half of 1953. In Moncton, the year began on a practical note with an increase in bus fares. The price of an adult ticket went from seven to ten cents, but a savings was offered at three tickets for a quarter. Children would henceforth pay five cents per trip, but six children's tickets would cost only twenty-five cents. Until then, they had sold ten for the same price. The new fares came into effect on Wednesday, January 14, the day after Radio-Canada's *Concerts du mardi* broadcast Darius Milhaud's Concerto no. 2, written for the violinist Arthur LeBlanc, and, in a Canadian première, played by the Acadian himself and accompanied by the Montréal Symphony Orchestra. During the first half of 1953, the violinist Arthur LeBlanc, the Acadian soldiers in Korea, and the Melanson triplets more or less accounted for Acadia's contribution to the international scene. As for the students of Saint-Joseph College who spent the winter rehearsing the *Bourgeois gentilhomme*, they went as far as Victoria, at the other end of the country, to participate in the Canadian Drama Festival, where they did win a prize, though not first place.

Life in Acadia was therefore quiet compared to the upheavals on the international front. When these events became too heavy to bear, one could always turn to the news briefs for a more human perspective on distant horizons. Two in particular captured the imagination of

Baby M.'s mother. In Toronto, a father offered to exchange his eyes for a house for his wife and six children, who were living in a garage. The man found a buyer, but the blind buyer, who "knew what it was to be blind," required only one eye from the unfortunate father, who had thought "blindness was preferable to poverty." The other news brief was about a London cab driver who did not like foreigners and who was fined eleven dollars "for refusing to accept an Arab sultan as a passenger." The man later gave up driving a cab when he learned that the sultan in question had been known to leave tips of 140 dollars.

Baby M.'s mother felt that a newspaper ought to deal with all facets of life, and enjoyed the fact that the entirely commonplace, such as an ad for Barbour products, appeared alongside the most extraordinary. It should be noted that Barbour provided something more or less universal, with its homogenized peanut butter, its prepared mustard, its jellied desserts in six flavours, and its double-action Acadia baking powder. Other advertisements punctuated the day-dreams of energy-drained housewives: Cream of the West and Five Roses fought the flour wars, Domestic peddled its lard, Kraft its Parkay margarine, Magic its baking powder, and Fleischman its yeast. As for tea and coffee, Chase & Sanborn, Nescafé, Salada, and King Cole offered no less than the best. But when it came to beverages, no one could match the genius of the H. F. Tennant distribution company of Church Street in combining the virtues of its product with life's circumstances. In the first place, the ad explained, Coke, which sold for seven cents a bottle, tax included, or thirty-six cents for a six-pack, went "well with any meal . . . whether right after a soup, a meat dish, or dessert" and "truly made good food taste better." The product, further-

more, attained the summit of perfection on special occa-
sions — at Easter, for example, when Coke tasted great with
baked ham. At the rate of an ad every two weeks, one could
learn not only about the beneficial effects of the drink with
the "world-wide reputation of quenching thirst fast," but
also about those tough times in life when, really, there
wasn't anything to do but drink a Coke. Whether the
"steering wheel starts to stick," or "your shopping seems to
take forever," or "the heat is unbearable," it was always
time for a Coke. In general, Coke was recommended
whenever there was loss of identity of any kind and a
reaffirmation of the self was required ("anytime you're
working, take a Coke break"). Canada Dry's ads ("every-
body's favourite!") were no match for H. F. Tennant's clear-
sighted advertising, whereas those of Sussex Ginger Ale, a
local manufacturer, simply asked for the return of empties
in order to ensure a continuous supply.

ↀ

L'Évangéline also did its part, in 1953, to warn people
against a sly new force, as dangerous as Communism or the
atomic bomb. The movies, with their enormous capacity to
influence the masses, were of concern to all institutions of
authority, including the Church, for whom the cinema,
along with newspapers and radio, had "knocked down the
signposts by which men could think according to their
ancestral beliefs and their national mind-set." Such language, with its references to familiar realities such as
signposts, ancestors, and nationalism, pulled on Acadian
heart-strings. Many therefore read the series of church-
inspired articles dealing with the irresistible power of the

seventh art. Possibly because the Church was also thinking of using this means of communication for its own ends, it was careful not to condemn the cinema outright, endeavouring instead to warn people against its pernicious side. According to the Church, by allowing the viewer to experience "generally forbidden or rejected emotions," movies created an interior malaise not easily overcome. A campaign of decontamination and education aimed therefore to educate Catholics by exhorting them to pay attention to the morality ratings and to abstain from seeing movies that were not recommended. The Church deplored the fact that too many Catholics regarded film morality ratings as good for others but not for themselves. As a result, far too many Catholics were venturing into theatres showing proscribed films.

Statements such as these tended to leave a shadow of doubt in the minds of those generally Catholic people such as Nurse Vautour and Baby M.'s mother, who did, as a matter of fact, consider themselves to be capable of mature judgement. Nevertheless, even such people were not always able to ignore the insinuations of the Church on the subject of human frailties. For religious authorities were warning the faithful against the movies' real dénouement, which plays itself out once the lights have come back on at the end of the feature and the spectator must quit the world of dreams and return to his or her own life, his or her own reality. In short, the Church did not believe the average man spiritually strong enough to return to the fold after a few hours of identifying with a film's brave hero, kissing "a beautiful star, whose powers of seduction sometimes far outmatched those of the housewife seated next to him." On the other hand, under the guise of entertainment, some movies could severely unnerve a viewer and, consequently, disrupt his peace of mind for several days thereafter. Other films, by offering recipes for emotional happiness which were marginally moral or based on material values, forced viewers into "a struggle against themselves in order to uphold Christian lifestyles." All things considered, the cinema could be a dangerous trap and, still according to the Church, rare were those who escaped its clutches. These repeated warnings often cited the archbishop of Paris Cardinal Feltin's words, prophesying that human beings would eventually pay dearly for expanding their consciousness.

⁊

In January 1953, there were four movie theatres in Moncton: the Empress, the Capitol, the Imperial, and the Paramount. All together, they showed some dozen films each week. There were also theatres in Shediac (the Capitol), Bouctouche (the Roxy), and Richibouctou (the Pine). Of course, the quasi-totality of movies came from the United States and were shown in English. *L'Évangéline* published daily listings of movies being shown in all these theatres. The list sometimes included the three Bathurst theatres (the Capitol, the Kent, and the Pines), the three Edmunston theatres (the Capitol, the Star, and the Martin), the Acadia of Saint-Léonard, and the Montcalm of Saint-Quentin. Monday's list was the longest, as it included movie showings through the following Saturday, the theatres being closed on Sunday. Each film was rated from one to four: a one rating indicated a movie was appropriate for general audiences, a two rating restricted it to mature adults, a three was ascribed to movies containing proscribed scenes, and a four to movies proscribed in their entirety. On the whole, the proportion of movies rated from one to three was equal. By no means were all the best American films of the early fifties shown in Moncton, but several ended up being projected in one or another of the city's theatres.

In response to Acadian popular demand in the Moncton area, the manager of the Empress theatre agreed to show French films once a week. Because there was only one showing per night, the evening took on a certain chic. *Rideau à 8 h 40* was inaugurated Wednesday, January 28, with *Fandango*, starring the incomparable Luis Mariano, whom Franco-Monctonians had already applauded in *Andalousie*, which had appeared in the same theatre the previous fall. *Nous irons à Paris* (*We're Off to Paris*), with Ray Ventura and his orchestra, Françoise Arnoul, Philippe Lemaire, and Pasquali, was shown the following week. Tickets for these two première presentations cost seventy-five cents for a seat in the orchestra and sixty-five cents for a spot in the balcony. Prices were reduced to sixty and fifty cents for subsequent shows, which featured *La Voyageuse inattendue* (*The Unexpected Traveller*), with Georges Marchal and Dany Robin; *Le Sorcier du ciel* (*The Sorcerer from the Sky*), the story of a saintly priest from Ars, or "Satan's struggle against a saint," with Georges Rollin; *L'héroïque Monsieur Boniface* (*The Heroic Mr. Boniface*), starring Fernandel and Liliane Bert; *Au Royaume des cieux* (*In the Kingdom of Heaven*), with Suzanne Cloutier; and *Je n'aime que toi* (*I Love Only You*), with Luis Mariano and Martine Carol. Some of these films were also shown at the Roxy in Bouctouche and the Pine in Richibouctou, where the program also included *Ma pomme* (*My Apple*), starring Maurice Chevalier; *La révoltée* (*The Rebel Girl*), with Victor Francen; and *Deux amours* (*Two Loves*), starring Tino Rossi. In these

Kent County theatres, showings began at 8:30, ten minutes earlier than in Moncton. Also, movies shown at the Roxy on Tuesday were screened at the Pine on Thursday. Judging by the movie listings in *l'Évangéline*, the Capitol in Shediac did not participate in this effort to show French films. But in June, it did show *Petite Aurore, l'enfant martyre* (*Little Aurore, the Martyred Child*), and, in December, it screened Vittorio de Sica's *Demain il sera trop tard* (*Tomorrow Will Be Too Late*), which had played in English at the Imperial in Moncton at the beginning of the year. Finally, near the end of the year, the Roxy in Bouctouche also took the initiative to show *Procès au Vatican* (*Trial in the Vatican*), a non-controversial film on the life of Saint Theresa, featuring a reconstruction of the Carmel nunnery and its ceremonies.

Though the screening of movies in French was certainly worthy of praise, it did pose certain problems. Baby M.'s father, committed scriptor that he was, had exposed these problems in one of his editorials. In essence, he argued that the operators of commercial theatres should not expect people to prostrate themselves with gratitude because the former had seen fit to show a French film when the print was so bad that the dialogue was barely comprehensible. The Acadian ear not being particularly attuned to the accents of, say, Fernandel, if people had to struggle with poor sound to boot, French movies in Moncton were destined for the sort of death that no advertising campaign could forestall. *L'Évangéline* applauded the showing of French films in Moncton, but not at the price of scratched prints in which the language was unrecognizable. Such mediocrity was likely to further strain the Acadian people's spirit of sacrifice (already stretched to the limit by Loyalist persistence and the tentacles of the American dream) and to turn them away once and for all from a French culture which they would end up remembering as indecipherable.

છ્ય

Criticism, whatever its object, is always more likely to be accepted when people feel that it is justified. This explains why it is generally based on facts. It also explains why selections for the Nobel Peace Prize and the Nobel Prize in literature are more often contested than those awarded in the scientific fields. Anyone with the ability to read can have an opinion on a literary work, and any minimally informed citizen may feel qualified to evaluate an international personality. The Nobel juries' decisions in the fields of chemistry, physics, and medicine and physiology, on the other hand, are more easily accepted, since few people consider themselves qualified to second-guess. It is also possible that the public is more indulgent towards scientists, because we have the feeling that they are really working, as opposed to writers, who often seem to be living the easy life, or those princes of peace, who seem to have a taste for good eating and travel. As a matter of fact, around 1953, the status of people working for peace had become somewhat muddied.

Winston Churchill, the last historian to receive the Nobel Prize in literature, was joined at the awards ceremony by General George Catlett Marshall, the first military man to be awarded the Nobel Peace Prize. General Marshall was recognized for having formulated the American aid plan for the reconstruction of Europe following the Second World War. The year before, the Nobel Peace Prize had gone to the musician and musicologist, theologian, philosopher, and French missionary Doctor Albert Schweitzer. In 1954,

1955, and again in 1956, no one was deemed worthy of the prize. It was not until 1957 that a sufficiently reassuring pacifist figure rose above the crowd: Canadian Lester B. Pearson, who had dedicated himself to international relations for forty years. It was in large part due to his talents that Canada gained the reputation of a country playing an active role to re-establish a lasting world peace. The efforts and qualities of Lester B. Pearson, a likeable, optimistic man with a keen mind, had notably contributed to the resolution of the Suez Canal crisis in 1956, a conflict that threatened to ignite a confrontation between the Soviet Union and the United States.

But needless to say, the complex relationship between Baby M. and the world was not restricted to literature and peace. All the sciences played a part. Both the 1953 Nobel Prize in chemistry, awarded to the German Hermann Staudinger for his work in macromolecular chemistry, and the 1952 award to two Brits, John Porter Martin and Richard Laurence Millington Synge, for perfecting chromatographic separation, recognized work with the potential to transform Baby M.'s life, or illness. The inventors of paper chromatography, a procedure to analyse substances in extremely small quantities, did much to advance our knowledge of amino acids, an essential component of living matter. In 1954, the Nobel Prize in chemistry went to the American Linus Carl Pauling, a pioneer in the study of chemical links and molecular structure. Starting out in quantum mechanics, Mr. Pauling subsequently turned his attention to the structure of crystals, resonance theory, protein structures, antibodies, hereditary diseases, anaesthesia, and vitamin C therapy. In 1962, he received the Nobel Peace Prize for his writings and conferences on the dangers of radioactive fallout.

As for the Nobel Prize in physics, it was awarded, in 1953, to the Dutchman Frits Zernike, who developed the technique for the observation of phases in contrast. This advancement in microscopy may also have influenced Baby M.'s life, since it was now possible to see bacteria and cells which had, until then, remained invisible. The previous year, the Nobel Prize in physics had gone to Felix Bloch, an American of Swiss origin, and to the American Edward Mills Purcell, for their work in nuclear magnetism. In 1954, it went to Max Born, an Englishman born in Germany, for his statistical interpretation of quantum theory. That same year, the Swedish Academy of Sciences also rewarded the German Walther Wilhelm Bothe, inventor of the technique of coincidences in the use of the Geiger counter. His work made a major impact on the corpuscular theory of light and on nuclear fission products.

The Nobel Prize in medicine or physiology was awarded in 1953 to Hans Adolf Krebs, a German with British citizenship, and to Fritz Albert Lipmann, a German-born American, for their metabolic studies. Krebs was recognized for his discovery of the citric acid cycle (the Krebs cycle), which describes the oxydization of pyruvic acid into carbon dioxide and water, but he had also studied other metabolic processes, particularly those relating to energy (a major issue of that time), as well as the ornithine cycle in the liver's biosynthesis of urea, and the glyoxylate cycle in the metabolism of lipids. Lipmann, for his part, was rewarded for his discovery of the coenzyme A and its importance in the intermediary metabolism. He concentrated mainly on classifying the phosphates which produce energy, but his research also led him to study the thyroid gland, fibroblasts and the Pasteur effect, glycolysis in the metabolisms of embryonic cells, and the mechanism of synthesis of peptides and proteins. In 1952, the Nobel Prize in medicine or physiology had been awarded to Selman Abraham Waksman, a Russian-born American, for his work on antibiotics effective in the treatment of tuberculosis. His other research dealt principally with the microbiology of soils and the sea. In 1954, the Americans John Franklin Enders, Frederick Chapman Robbins, and Thomas Huckle Weller shared the Nobel Prize in medicine or physiology for having discovered that the poliomyelitis virus could be cultivated in various types of tissues. Their work led to the perfection of a vaccine against the deadly tuberculosis bacterium.

Even though, in the beginning, Alfred Nobel intended his prizes to go to the most extraordinary achievements of the year, those that were eventually responsible for awarding them realized that a degree of hindsight was required in order to judge the true scope of a work or discovery. This difficulty was particularly acute in the scientific fields, where one had to verify a new theory's application. Thus, for example, the scientists who won the Nobel Prizes in 1953 were recognized for research the results of which had been published several years earlier. Similarly, two Brits and one American who published the results of their work on heredity in 1953 were only awarded the Nobel Prize in medicine or physiology in 1962. Francis Harry Compton Crick, Maurice Hugh Frederick Wilkins, and James Dewey Watson had discovered the double-helix structure of the deoxyribonucleic acid molecule in chromosomes (DNA) and its duplication process during mitosis. This discovery opened the way to understanding the crucial role of DNA as a transmitter of information in living matter. They identified the two essential functions of DNA: *transmitting* the parent cells' code to the descendants while, at the same time, *expressing* this code through the organization of protein synthesis.

❧

A man with no small regard for literature, the Moncton pediatrician who was treating Baby M. to the best of his ability finally succeeded in snatching her from the jaws of death. He had taken his inspiration from, among other things, a recently published American book on celiac disease. The book contained photographs of babies in the critical stages of the illness (shrivelled buttocks and thighs, morose, glassy eyes), along with photos of these same children as adults. The adults appeared relatively normal, if slightly overweight. The doctor showed these pictures to Baby M.'s mother, who derived some hope from them. This same book also provided information suggesting that Baby M.'s recovery was highly probable, the illness having been diagnosed in time. In spite of all this, Baby M. was not reacting to treatment as well as had been hoped. She was taking longer than expected to gain strength and to control her incontinence. Finally, after a dozen days of closely monitored care, and not knowing what else to do, the doctor visited Baby M.'s parents to inform them of the situation. He explained that it was a question of days. If Baby M. did not begin to react positively to the treatment, they should expect the worst. The committed scriptor felt his throat go dry and saw his wife — queen and martyr — turn pale.

In the end, Baby M. survived celiac disease. The Moncton pediatrician's foresight certainly had a great deal to do with it, but it may well be that his calmness in the face of the possible ravages of *Writing Degree Zero* played an even greater part. This imperturbability alone ought to have earned him the Nobel Prize in medicine or physiology. Of course, the doctor expected no such reward; he did not even imagine the case would have some future literary return. He was too busy saving the primary life to think of the other, the one that looks back on itself in order to fling itself that much farther ahead. The scientific and medical journals were piled up on his desk, burying the double-helix structure of DNA beneath the mess. How could he imagine that Baby M. would live doubly or that, through her, he would do likewise? Like Alfred Nobel through his prizes. Like Nurse Vautour through the handsome Gregory Peck. Like Baby M.'s mother through her dumbfounded children staring at the tongues of clothing emerging from the rollers of her new washing-machine. Like Baby M.'s father before the daily miracle of *l'Évangéline* newspaper. Like Brigitte transfixed by the power of her backhand. Like Élizabeth floating in the amniotic fluid of love. Like Claude in the never-ending risk of the body.

6

Idle Talk and Composition II

An inescapable internal rectitude — Bishop of Besançon in spite of himself — Monctonian parallel between the coronation of Elizabeth II and the sinking of the Titanic — Willie Lamothe and his Musical Rodeo in Dieppe — Sunrise over Acadia — A movie is blacklisted — Christine Jorgensen's transformation — Where body and soul are one — The concept of professional virginity and Marian coincidences in Acadia — Once more the Te Deum — Nurse Vautour and the last train of the season to Pointe-du-Chêne

C L A U D E . In 1953, Claude was three years old. He lived in France and had knowledge of neither Acadia nor Montréal. He had no doubt heard of the Jews. He had perhaps heard of *Writing Degree Zero*. His father, an eminent psychiatrist, may have rubbed shoulders with Roland Barthes himself. Not being the son of a geographer, at the age of three, Claude knew nothing of the sound barrier and the two Jacquelines, but he did, in a sense, fall within Françoise Dolto's field of observation.

Claude. The androgynous nature of this name already evokes a certain resonance. And if Claude seemed to have slipped away after awakening feelings of love in Élizabeth, he did not do so limping (the Latin *Claudus* meaning "one who limps," from which is derived the French *claudiquer*, that is "to limp"). On the contrary, he distanced himself in response to a kind of internal rectitude. In this, he behaved not unlike his patron saint, Saint Claude, a solitary priest of the seventh century who had been unwillingly appointed Bishop of Besançon. After a while, no longer able to bear the responsibilities to which he had been assigned, the bishop finally fled, only, alas, to be recaptured and forced back to his post. Five years later, once again exasperated by the "constraints of his vocation," the future Saint Claude resigned and went off to live in a monastery in Jura. Unfortunately for him, he was once again chosen to be a leader of men, this time in the role of Father Abbot. The independent fire and free spirit of Saint Claude have lost nothing of their ardour in the twentieth-century Claude, whom we now find once again sitting in a bar.

In *Real Life*, Claude met a woman in a Berlin bar who inspired him to explore the art of massage more deeply. The woman said absolutely nothing about the subject, but their meeting profoundly convinced Claude that it ought to be possible to gain access to the soul through touching the body. For a long time nothing had seemed more important to Claude than increasing his understanding — while raising others' awareness — of the particular workings of memory and desire, the action of the two being intermingled rather than distinct. He had arrived at the conclusion that this, and nothing else, was what life was about, and that memory and desire are nothing without each other, just as the body is nothing without the soul and vice versa. Claude had personally undertaken this research, if we may be permitted to use the term, quite naturally, outside of any context. It had become the thread of his existence, a thread which, sooner or later, always seemed to lead him back to a bar. This might take a few days, or several weeks, or months. There was no rule. Only something like a thirst lurking on the edges of time.

ℰᴏ

For Acadians in the Moncton area, 1953 could be divided into two periods of almost equal duration. International events dominated the first half of the year, up until the coronation of Elizabeth II, whereas local accomplishments occupied centre stage during the second half of the year. The demolition of the Imperial theatre on Main Street, only days after the coronation, might serve as a demarcation between the two periods. It must be said that, in Moncton, the celebrations to mark Elizabeth II's accession to the head of the Empire revealed a rather troubling ambiguity. Alhough, at times, festivities were quite inoffensive — afternoon teas, for example — they also took on a rather funereal bent with the showing, at the Capitol, of the movie *The Titanic*. As an added value, the film about the sinister sinking was screened precisely at midnight — that is, at the first hour of coronation day.

That summer something of a circus atmosphere prevailed. On the one hand, la Société l'Assomption boasted record insurance sales, while, on the other, preparations were under way in Dieppe to host Willie Lamothe and his Musical Rodeo. He was soon followed by John Diefenbaker, Lester B. Pearson, and the King Bros. and Cristiani Circus. In August, on the show *Singing Stars of Tomorrow*, young opera singers Dolorès Nowlan and Marie-Germaine LeBlanc proved themselves worthy descendants of the great Acadian singer Anna Malenfant, whose voice, it was said, rivalled only a winter sunset or Gabrielle Roy's *La Petite poule d'eau*. During the summer, it was also announced that Canadian slums were of higher quality than those in the United States, and that Marie, "the prettiest and 'youngest' " of the Dionne quintuplets, would become a contemplative nun. These months of effervescence turned out to be a fine prelude to the fall, which offered Acadians reason to rejoice in the prospects of their modest nation's ambitions.

The upsurge operated both on the material and on the ideological planes, with concrete achievements and soaring spirits having an equal impact. It was as though the consolidation of the Empire around a new queen had also inspired Acadians to unite around their own noble institutions. In this respect, September made a powerful impact. Such an impact, in fact, that it actually struck a day early, on Monday, August 31, 1953, with the consecration of His Excellency Monsignor Albert Leménager, first bishop of the diocese of Yarmouth. This Acadian version of Elizabeth II's coronation reverberated loudly throughout Acadia. Prepared, as always, to defend *l'Évangéline*'s role as "the Acadian people's national newspaper," Baby M.'s father spared no effort in covering the magnificent gathering, which took place nearly two hundred years after the Deportation. Baby M., who was approaching her seventh month of gestation, was not unmoved by the reddish glow that resembled a rising sun over

Acadia. But there was little room to rejoice in the increasingly restricted space of her mother's womb.

☙

So powerful was September's impact that it struck a second time at the end of August, when Moncton's Capitol theatre screened the sacrilegious movie of the year, Otto Preminger's *The Moon Is Blue*. The film had caused controversy both in the United States and Canada. At the time of its release, the archbishop of Washington had proclaimed, in no uncertain terms, that "from time to time, Catholics are faced with a challenge, and this film is one such challenge. It is up to us to have sufficient conviction to abstain, thereby demonstrating that, for a great many of us, the moon is blue because blue is the colour of the Holy Virgin, to whom these lines from the *Song of Songs* apply: 'beautiful as the moon, brilliant as the stars, terrible as an army deployed for battle.'" According to the major Catholic journal the *Sign*, the movie, which was intended to be funny, contained so much coarse language that it was disgusting, "burying any beauty in an avalanche of double entendres, without regard for common Christian morality." In New Brunswick, where only a fraction of American films worthy of note were ever shown, the movie was screened thanks to a court of law, which annulled the provincial censor's interdiction.

It is worth noting that the director who dared to make *The Moon Is Blue* had actually earned doctorates in law and philosophy. Son of a Viennese lawyer of some notoriety, Otto Preminger had taken an early interest in the stage, and worked as an assistant to famed theatre director Max Reinhardt even before completing his studies. Having earned some success as a theatre director himself, Preminger made his first movie in 1931, at the age of twenty-five. He subsequently went to work on Broadway, where one of Hollywood's big studios snapped him up. He worked in both the theatre and film for a while, before dedicating himself exclusively to the cinema. Part of a trend with Lubitsch and Mankiewicz, Preminger-the-filmmaker achieved a kind of high point with *Angel Face* (1952), his fourteenth movie since his arrival in America. The change of tone which was to follow was not unrelated to the fact that Preminger had become an independent producer, entirely free of the big film studios. In bringing to the screen *The Moon Is Blue*, a play which had won rave reviews on Broadway, he was exploiting this freedom in order to "defy rigid American censorship." The words "professional virgin," "seduction," and "mistress," which were spoken several times during the movie, had never been heard before in the cinema.

The Catholic Centre for Cinema, which rated all films available for screening in France, recognized the comic side of *The Moon Is Blue*. It noted that Preminger's film was "punctuated with humour and enhanced by sparkling dialogue." However, the Centre regretfully added, the plot line "might have avoided dire consequences if, under the guise of comedy, true values and moral principles had not been continually ridiculed." The film was given a 4B rating, which meant people were advised against seeing it, because it could only "harm the majority of adults and damage the spiritual and moral health of society." The cinematic rating system to which *l'Évangéline* adhered expressed the same reservations, but, since the range of classification was less subtle, *The Moon Is Blue* simply fell into the category of totally proscribed movies. Of all the movies that played in Moncton in 1953, it was the only one to be so classified. Another such rare case arose the following year, in March, as Baby M., who was eighteen weeks old, was busy preparing her celiac crisis. The movie *Martin Luther* would be judged "harmful and positively bad . . . a moral and social danger."

⁊

The blacklisting of the film *The Moon Is Blue* certainly caused some agitation, but not as much as the incredible transformation of Christine Jorgensen. The secrecy surrounding this amazing affair was first broached at the end of 1952 by a journalist from the *Daily News*, a New York tabloid, but the whole truth only emerged several months later, in April 1953, at the end of the second month of Baby M.'s gestation. The baby's sex had already been determined by then, but no one could as yet be certain that the glands and sexual organs of the fetus would develop into those of a girl or boy. This lack of transparency was related, as a matter of fact, to the problem of the young George Jorgensen, who turned to Danish science in order to transform his appearance so that it might better reflect his deeper sexual identity. The treatment would require several stages, but already in June 1952, the twenty-six-year-old ex-GI had become a ravishing Christine, living a normal life in the Danish capital and pursuing a career as a photographer. From her/his home in Copenhagen, George/Christine had written his parents to tell them he was undergoing treatment in order to correct a physiological problem that had distorted his true sexual identity. The goal, he explained, was to allow his hidden feminine nature to blossom fully.

The operation may have had little impact on Danish society (several Danish journalists were aware of the affair but agreed not to speak of it), but it electrified America. In a single week, the three main American news agencies regurgitated in excess of fifty thousand words on the topic. Journalists descended on Copenhagen, attempting by various means to get inside the hospital room where Christine was recovering from one of the numerous operations necessary to her transformation. Either in person or by transatlantic telephone, journalists posed every imaginable question. They even wanted to know whether Christine wore pyjamas or a nightgown, if her interests were masculine or feminine . . . in other words, whether she enjoyed baseball or knitting. *Time* and *Newsweek* did their best to explain the affair. They published details on the transformation process (five major surgeries and one minor, and more than two thousand hormone injections), described in great detail the frenzy of the journalists covering the story, and reported that medical specialists throughout the world felt the media tumult over the sexual transformation was laughable. These specialists claimed that transsexualization was far from a rare operation, and even quite common in several hospitals in the United States. *Time* went so far as to explore the nomenclature of the procedure, attempting to define for the public at large the terms *hermaphroditism* and *pseudohermaphroditism*, both perfectly respectable anomalies compared with *homosexuality*, which, for its part, was in no way congenital, in spite of some homosexuals' claims to the contrary. The article went on to explain that, among other things, homosexuals refused psychiatric treatments intended to offer them a chance at a normal life.

Time also managed to establish that some homosexuals had well and truly attempted to convince American surgeons to transform them into pseudowomen, but that the majority of these doctors refused any involvement in what was a crime against nature as well as the laws of forty-eight states.

℘

Claude. This time the bar in question is located in Toronto. Is the kitsch of the decor intentional or accidental? There is no way of knowing. Nor is it any easier to define the sort of people that gather here. The point is that they gather. They may be young or old, but they are all more or less the same age, the age of the slightly worn-out soul, the soul that wants to live, but not at any price. Because nothing here seems to be prepared to live at any price. Nothing wants to spring forth, nothing absolutely needs to erupt. At least not in those terms. People's sexuality, for example, does not seem to have that primordial need to spring forth.

And yet, bodies play a critical role in this place. As a group, they produce movement, distribute atmosphere. Individually, they attract the eye, move the spirit. Here and there, people stand, walk, or look around. Others are seated. Some talk quietly, some are more determined. More determining. At least in comparison to the rest of the scene. At least in comparison to the calm that envelops everything. If someone were to burst out laughing, for example, they would immediately hear their own noise. Would immediately become conscious of it. Although there are times when noise is welcome. Like music, for instance. When it does not seek to crush or restrict anything. Particularly spontaneity. With a burst of laughter. A fit of jealousy. An outburst of anger. Because all things can live. Ought to live. Emerging from within to the external world without ever worrying or shocking. Because body and soul are one.

Claude has been seated for approximately an hour at the end of the long bar. A while ago, another man sat down nearby. They are separated by a single stool. They have exchanged a few words. They are quiet, more or less united in this activity which consists of watching people circulate in the large room. As they make small-talk, Claude tells the stranger he is a masseur, but that he is just about to give up the profession. More to maintain the gentle rhythm of their conversation than out of any real interest, the other man asks him why. Claude shrugs. The other man does not pursue the matter. He has no desire to become entangled in answers. In any case, there probably is no answer. The two men fall silent. The to and fro of the room gently rocks their gazes and their thoughts. Until something comes to an end. Claude empties his glass and pays the barman. Before leaving, he hands his business card to the man who is no longer entirely a stranger and, without another word, walks out of the situation.

℘

No Girl at All. America, which had clung desperately to the notion that George's transformation into Christine was in fact merely the finishing touches to a work of Nature, was finally obliged to face the facts: George Jorgensen had clearly been a male, which made Christine (now *the* belle of Manhattan, rubbing shoulders with celebrities and playing to the media circus) a reworked male. There were those who argued that George/Christine had never implied the contrary, and many intelligent readers had long ago realized that there was nothing female about the original George Jorgensen. Such people sought to distance themselves from those who, shocked by the unthinkable, had attempted, in this case, to soften the blow by imagining a technical defect or natural anomaly of some sort that required the attention of the medical world.

Determined to get to the bottom of the case once and for all, the *New York Post* sent a correspondent to Denmark to meet Jorgensen's doctors, including a psychiatrist. The doctors were frank and open: Jorgensen was neither a hermaphrodite nor a pseudohermaphrodite. It was because of his fervent desire to live as a woman that he had been given the treatments necessary for his physical transformation. Jorgensen's psychiatrist, Dr. Georg Stuerup, added that psychiatry was practically powerless to deter true homosexuals from their preference. In response to the cries of alarm from American psychiatrists, according to whom transsexuals were risking even greater suffering than homosexuals (their transformation being illusory), the Danish doctors argued that the media frenzy surrounding transsexualization constituted a greater danger for their client than the transformation itself. Jorgensen's psychiatrist went so far as to describe the American attitude as puerile and hypocritical. He declared that transsexualization was a common practice in the United States and denounced American surgeons who were used to intervening on all parts of the human body, including the brain, but were not prepared to touch the testicles. It was the maturity of Danish society, he observed, that preserved it from such incongruity. He added that Danes would continue their work in the area of transsexualization, but without treating foreigners, since that provoked too much hysteria. Needless to say, this announcement was a great disappointment to the six hundred foreigners who had flocked to the doors of Danish medical science since the Jorgensen story had broken.

❧

As though by magic, the consecration of His Excellency Monsignor Albert Leménager shed some small light on the sacrilege committed by the movie *The Moon Is Blue*. His Excellency Monsignor Norbert Robichaud, archbishop of Moncton, hit the nail on the head in a sermon recalling the religious and Marian origins of ancient Acadia. He reminded everyone that the French colonial settlement of Acadia had coincided with the golden age of religious practice in France, a period that saw the birth of the French religious school of Cardinal de Bérulle. The Father of Conden, Saint Vincent de Paul, Monsieur Olier, Saint Jean Eudes, and Saint Louis-Marie de Montfort were the principal adepts of this spiritual school. The archbishop also recalled that Acadia had been founded during the reign of Louis XIII, a monarch who, "in 1630, had instructed that Mary be solemnly declared celestial protector of all his lands, and on August 15 of that same year, dedicated his realm and colonies to the Assumption of the Blessed Virgin Mary." According to Monsignor Robichaud, this explained both "the robust faith professed by our ancestors" and the "uninterrupted series of Marian events and coincidences" which had marked Acadian history.

Aside from this historical perspective on the religious fervour and torment of the 1755 Deportation, which was proof positive that God had not forgotten the Acadians (dixit the Angel to Tobias: ". . . it is because you have been agreeable to God, that you must be tested"), the consecration of His Excellency Monsignor Leménager was the occasion for the modern Acadia of 1953 to show itself in all its splendour. The event took on such importance that people referred to it simply as the consecration, the way they referred simply to the coronation, without having to mention who it was that was actually taking holy orders. Without a doubt, this gift offered by the Church to the Acadians of Baie-Sainte-Marie of "a bishop born on its soil, nourished in its homes, fortified in the shadow of its churches, educated in the spirit of a past renewing itself in glorious purity" was like a corner of heaven come down to earth. The jubilation and magnificence of the ceremonies culminated with the singing of the "Te Deum" and the "Ave Maris Stella" in Saint-Ambroise Cathedral in Yarmouth.

The incomparable ceremony of consecration was echoed in an equally extraordinary scene outside the cathedral. First, a great number of ex-parishioners, priests, and nuns had come from every corner of the Maritimes to join the faithful in the diocese of Yarmouth for the celebrations. Many participated, in one way or another, in the various parades (accompanied by the Cornwallis naval base band) and processions (including up to three hundred cars). As these passed, people kneeled at their doors to receive the Episcopal blessing. Others waved Acadian flags. The route was beautifully decorated. At one point, the official car stopped to allow the new bishop to accept a bouquet of flowers. In addition to the numerous receptions replete with appropriate speeches, there was a banquet complete with toasts and an elegant menu: celery, nuts, and olives; fruit bowls; consommé; lobster à la crème with a roll; roast turkey stuffed with jellied cranberries; mashed potatoes; peas and carrots in butter; ice cream, chocolate delights from Baie-Sainte-Marie, and Acadian cake; coffee and sodas; and finally, cigars and cigarettes.

҂

Sunday, August 30, 1953, on the eve of the consecration, Nurse Vautour waits peacefully, in the Moncton station, for the Sunday train to Pointe-du-Chêne. She has decided to take advantage of her day off and catch the season's last train to the Shediac beaches. The train leaves Moncton at half past noon and will quit Pointe-du-Chêne after supper, at 6:30. Nurse Vautour will spend the afternoon strolling through the village streets, along the dock and the beach. She has brought a sandwich, which, with the addition of some french fries or an ice cream cone, or both, she will make into a meal. In her travel bag there is also a pair of sneakers (she does not want to be seen wearing sneakers on the train), a sweater, a towel, her wallet, a bottle of *Tulipe noire* perfume, and the latest issue of the *Reader's Digest*. She is wearing a summer hat, purchased on sale at Vogue's and, for the first time, a new brand of nylons, which she picked up at a good price at Surette's drugstore.

Nurse Vautour arrives at the station three quarters of an hour early. She likes to watch the travellers coming and going, and the people on their way, like her, to picnic for the day. Absent-mindedly, she picks up a magazine on the bench beside her, leafs through it without conviction, her attention drawn mainly to the feverish activity of the waiting room. She is not really able to read until a kind of quiet settles over the waiting passengers. She reads that a reputed scholar, a Dr. Kinsey, is about to publish the results of his research on female sexuality in the United States. As far as she can make out, the conclusions of the study deal with the sort of morals depicted in *The Moon Is Blue*. As a matter of fact, the film is temporarily off the screen, until the Capitol begins showing it again later in the week.

Nurse Vautour has not yet decided if she will see *The Moon Is Blue*, the movie "that every Catholic should abstain from seeing." Although she finds all this talk of morality annoying, she is not willing to defy the Church openly. Happily, such dilemmas are not frequent. Because Nurse Vautour enjoys the movies. Unmarried and therefore relatively free to do as she pleases, she can go to the movies as often as she likes. On that score, Nurse Vautour can't help but pity Nurse Comeau who, because her shift begins at suppertime, cannot go to the movies during the week. But, as Nurse Comeau does not seem to realize what she is missing, Nurse Vautour does not dwell on it. She has no desire to appear the luckier of the two. Nurse Vautour is well aware of her good fortune and rarely envies other women's lives. All things considered, her life seems to her the best possible.

7

Real Life II

Comfortable swivelling stools made of chrome and plastic — A novelistic sense of time — Rain of death from the firmament — Cinematic and nuclear atmosphere in Hampton — Murmurings of an expectant mother — Intermission at the Kinsey's — The splendour of uranium — Mass defect, the nuclear family, and sexuality — Indestructible immortality — A destiny fulfilled even as it is revealed — Real versus virtual population of the world — Postmodern delinquency and other nuclear moments

THE IMPACT of September 1953 was further intensified seven days after the consecration, when Acadia became the scene of yet another apotheosis. In addition to celebrating its fiftieth anniversary that fall, the Société Mutuelle l'Assomption insurance company moved into its newly constructed four-story building on the corner of St. George and Archibald streets in Moncton. The various contractors involved in the work bought ads in a special insert published by *l'Évangéline* in honour of the event. The contractor Abbey Landry (the Dieppe, Lakeburn, and Parkton churches, Notre-Dame d'Acadie College, Moncton Fish Market) had directed the construction of the Shediac stone building, while the masonry contract was awarded to Donald Gould (the Brunswick Hotel, Eaton's) and the plastering to Abbey Cormier (Woolworth's and the Imperial Bank). Every effort was made to ensure the building would serve as a powerful symbol of Acadia in Moncton. Even the buttons on the elevator had been coded in French (OP for *ouvrir porte*, FP for *fermer porte*, SS for *sous-sol* and RC for *rez-de-chaussée*). To occupy the building, L'Assomption had attracted renters who shared its dedication to the glory of Acadia. Radio-Canada and the Provincial Bank shared the ground floor with Chez Marcil, which was equipped to feed its fine clientele on "comfortable swivelling stools made of chrome and plastic, and arranged around three horseshoe-shaped tables covered in red Formica, all of which comes together in a great look." As the mason Gould put it, "it takes good buildings to make good business."

The Acadian effervescence of September 1953 coincided with the start of a critical stage for Baby M., for whom there remained only two months of intra-uterine life. During this period, she would have to watch her weight and her cerebral life. A shortage of vitamins and mineral salts could damage her cerebral development. Baby M.'s extra-uterine life depended on these last two months. Circumstances, therefore, required Baby M. to gradually adapt to the stress of living. In addition to supervising her own development, she had to remember to press from time to time on the bladder and diaphragm of her mother, who required such occasional inconveniences in order to experience her pregnancy as normal. This was also the time for Baby M. to enter into a relationship marked by the anxiety of separation with her mother. All these behaviours had to be well regulated, so as not to upset or tire her mother unnecessarily, because, sooner or later, that could only harm Baby M. In the end, all these concerns contributed to Baby M.'s acquiring, in spite of herself, a sense of rhythm, which may well have already been a novelistic sense of time, a sense manifested in all its splendour on the day of her arrival, in the form of a so-called normal presentation, which is to say, head first.

❧

The possibility that scientists were on the verge of perfecting a new super-bomb, compared to which the A- (for atomic) bomb and the H- (for hydrogen) bomb "would be mere firecrackers," somewhat disrupted the calm which Baby M.'s mother had been working to preserve during the last two months of her pregnancy. The concept behind this C- (for cobalt) bomb was not reassuring. "An atomic bomb would be used to detonate a hydrogen bomb. The hydrogen bomb would be thickly encased in cobalt. The cobalt would become radioactive, and its dust would spread high up in the atmosphere. Atmospheric currents would spread this deadly dust throughout the universe. Then, a rain of death would slowly descend from the heavens onto every part of the globe. This poison would contaminate all its inhabitants. Men, women, and children would fall victim to the radioactivity and slowly die." This gloomy description in *l'Évangéline* was all the more troubling since many important countries, the United States and the USSR first among them, were falling over each other in their haste to announce that they possessed these impressive weapons. In spite of all the warnings against nuclear weapons by enlightened men and women (Mrs. Vijaya Lakshmi Pandit, sister of India's Prime Minister Nehru, had just been elected to the chairmanship of the United Nations, Mr. Pearson having been vetoed by the Russians), the apocalyptic bombs continued to gain ground from week to week. By the end of September, the United States was in a position to envisage the low-cost manufacture of H-bombs, thanks to its enormous plutonium factory in Aiken, South Carolina, which was ready to begin production. There was one catch, however: the Americans were short of modern military planes capable of transporting the bombs over long distances — to Russia, for example. On the other hand, although the Russians trailed the United States in terms of numbers of bombs, they were not lacking in planes to transport them.

Here was a scenario to worry a pregnant woman, especially when, since the beginning of the year, *l'Évangéline* had been reporting all the details of the American nuclear tests being conducted on the Yucca plains, explosions which shook the desert and cast a fiery light that could be seen for hundreds of miles. Even as certain details provided a clear picture of the impact ("cars parked thirty-five miles from the sight vibrated for four-and-a-half minutes after the explosion"), the American testers also announced grave plans. It was their intention to fly radar-controlled airplanes carrying mice and monkeys through the nuclear cloud, to plant a forest of pines, to build steel bridges, and to run a freight train through the test site, all to measure the effects of the blast. During the fall, nuclear proliferation spread first to Germany and Great Britain (which conducted its tests in Australia), and then underwater, with the launching of the first atomic-powered submarine. Canada played its part, providing the terrain for guided missile tests along the border between Saskatchewan and Alberta.

Though Acadia seemed to be free of the arms race, it was not entirely untouched. The nuclear fever had catapulted uranium into a position among precious metals formerly occupied by gold. As a result, for the previous five years, every uranium find had provoked another rush. As of the spring of 1953, the fever had struck various regions in Québec, the Sault Ste. Marie area, British Columbia, Saskatchewan, and Cape Breton. At last, at summer's end, it reached New Brunswick. On August 31, next to the article describing Monsignor Leménager's arrival in his future diocese of Yarmouth, *l'Évangéline* reported the discovery of what was believed to be a rich deposit of uranium in Hampton, not far from Saint John, upon which "an army of mining engineers and prospectors" had descended. "The scene, in this sleepy little town in King's County resembles a movie version of a gold rush. . . . People everywhere, elbow-to-elbow with ardent young engineers hurrying to the site to take samples of the precious element, in order to determine its potency." This cinematic allusion, along with the conclusion of the article (which implied that Hampton might become a flourishing city like Bathurst, where a major mineral deposit had been discovered), gave cause to rejoice and an opportunity to forget the nuclear threat for a few days. Baby M. observed all this fuss from within the uterus, which protected her from her environment without isolating her. She was not exactly sure what was causing all the excitement, but she did notice that this was a different agitation from the sort that usually quickened her mother's heartbeat, and which was generally followed by a raising of her voice. Baby M. did not yet know that four sisters and brothers had preceded her in the maternal womb and that, since their emergence, they had much to do with the greater or lower intensity of her mother's heartbeat.

&

Gazing out the window of the train, Nurse Vautour muses as she allows herself to be rocked to the rhythm of the rails. She has just finished reading the article on the researcher Kinsey in the magazine she picked up from the bench in the station. Dr. Kinsey's conclusions on the sexuality of American women somewhat disappointed her. As far as she can tell, any reasonable person could have arrived at the same conclusions, minus the statistics. What she does find interesting is Alfred Kinsey's career. A tireless worker, his social life was limited to Sunday evening musical get-togethers in his home. Dr. Kinsey, a dedicated musicologist, presented a program of classical music, commenting on each piece as it was played. Ladies were permitted to knit with muted needles at these recitals. During the intermission (cake and sherbet), the guests would converse about the pieces they had heard. Several people in the small university town of Bloomington who had initially felt honoured to be invited, eventually stopped attending these evenings, as they became annoyed at their host's intensity.

Alfred Charles Kinsey, born in New Jersey before the turn of the century, was a typical example of the American self-made man. Beginning as a workshop assistant in the Stevens Institute of Technology, he eventually became its director of mechanical sciences, and this even though he had spent almost all of the first ten years of his life in bed, suffering from rickets, heart trouble, and a case of typhoid fever that almost killed him. In the end, their son's numerous illnesses convinced the Kinseys to flee the polluted air of Hoboken and settle in the country, which greatly benefitted little Alfred's health. In the country, of course, the boy discovered a multitude of flowers and birds. But his curiosity for nature was only truly sparked when one day he discovered a flower which did not appear in the botany book his father had given him. Alfred's study on the behaviour of birds in the rain was published while he was still in grammar school. The young man completed his high school with excellent results, and without having neglected his piano. While at Harvard, Alfred Kinsey studied comestible wild plants of North America. He was subsequently fascinated by cynips, whose curious biological characteristics constituted proof in his eyes that evolution was not completed. Accompanied by his wife and children, he travelled over eighty thousand miles to gather three-and-a-half million specimens (the cynips is a parasitic insect living exclusively on oak trees), and compiled a mountain of statistics. He was forty-four years old when some students questioned him on the sexual behaviour of married couples. That was all it took. Ten years later, he published the results of his research on the sexual behaviour of the American male. A similar study on female sexuality was about to be released and Catholic authorities had already placed it on the black list.

ح

In 1789, the German scientist Martin Heinrich Klaproth coined the name *uranium* (after the planet Uranus, sighted for the first time eight years earlier) for this "unknown substance which behaves like a metal." Some forty years later, the Frenchman Eugène Melchior provided some additional facts about uranium without, however, awakening any great interest in the element. Approximately fifty years would pass before Henri Becquerel discovered the radioactive properties of uranium. Then, in 1898, the work of Pierre and Marie Curie (née Sklodowska) led to the discovery of two new elements in the same family as uranium: polonium (from Poland, Madame Curie's homeland) and radium (thus named for its radioactive properties). At the time, Madame Curie was the only woman to have received the Nobel Prize, winning it in physics in 1903 jointly with her husband Pierre and M. Becquerel. Marie Curie was also the first person to be Nobelized twice, winning the Nobel Prize in chemistry on her own in 1911, for her discovery of Po and Ra, and for her additional work in radioactivity.

Until the Second World War, the element U would be employed mainly as a source for radium, used in the treatment of cancer. Uranium salts, which are phosphorescent, were also added to glass, to facilitate the observation of ultraviolet rays. But uranium, the sole element in nature whose nucleus is fissionable by slow neutrons, only truly came into its own in 1938, with the discovery of nuclear fission, the energy chain reaction which is the basis of the atomic bomb. The discovery of nuclear fission was the result of Einstein's work and his intuition of the *mass defect*, that incredible force which binds neutrons in the atom's nucleus. According to Grolier's *Livre des connaissances*, a mass defect of one gram corresponds approximately to the amount of heat required to transform 220,000 tons of ice into vapour. Many scientists were responsible for concretizing the nuclear potential based on Einstein's theories and the work of Hahn and Strassman in Germany, Frisch and Meitner in Denmark, the Joliot-Curies in France, and the Italian Fermi in the United States.

As astonishing as uranium and nuclear fission turned out to be, they were soon overshadowed by the discovery of nuclear fusion, which led to the hydrogen bomb. To understand the magnitude of the H-bomb, one need only recall that the Hiroshima atomic bomb — which killed 72,000 people and completely flattened an area of twelve square kilometres — contained a mere kilogram of uranium, which is the equivalent of about one thousand tons of T.N.T. And yet, this tremendous force would serve as a mere match to ignite the hydrogen bomb, also called the thermonuclear bomb, because a temperature of at least fifty million degrees Celsius is required to trigger nuclear fusion. To describe the phenomenon another way, suffice it to say that nuclear fusion is the source of the sun's energy, no less. As for the incomparable power of the C-bomb, it results from the triplet fission-fusion-fission, all contained under the same roof, in a manner of speaking.

The first experimental explosion of a hydrogen bomb occurred on October 31, 1952, in the Marshall Islands, a territory of the United States in the Pacific Ocean. The bomb weighed 67 tons and was 125 times more powerful than the one dropped on Hiroshima. The test raised the possibility of a more efficient mechanism of the same type completely wiping out all of humanity in a single stroke. In spite of this, Baby M., whose soul was already wandering the earth, decided to enter into gestation. All that remained was to select a family and a sex. As innocent as the choice of family might seem, it was not easy, given the important role family ties had played in the perfection of the nuclear bomb. Think of the couple Pierre and Marie Curie, of their daughter Irene, who, together with Frédéric Joliot, formed the team of Joliot-Curie; of the Austrian Lise Meitner and her nephew Otto Frisch, and of the Rosenbergs, to name a few. As for choosing a sex, it was no easier than choosing a family, judging from the Jorgensen affair, which had plunged sexual identity, along with the rest of the globe, into the fiery cauldron of degeneration and reconstitution.

ೞ

The train's motion and the progress of Dr. Kinsey's life have plunged Nurse Vautour into a kind of cinematic reverie. This woman in her fifties watched the scientist's life take shape before her eyes as she read the article while the landscape filed past. Now she feels a certain lightness, as though she were detached from reality, as though she were at the movies. She feels good. Floating effortlessly above matter and reality, she does not feel the effort of the locomotive carrying her so easily through space. This lightness has a virtuous feel to it, like an emanation floating high above everything. To put it bluntly, she feels free and immortal. She needs nothing, desires nothing more.

It may have been theoretically possible, in 1953, to elim-inate all feelings of immortality, but this had not yet been done. Cardinal Stepinac, Lavrenti Beria, and Baby M. are prime examples. Cardinal Stepinac, under arrest in the Krasic territory of Yugoslavia, continued to berate his coun-try's Communists, proclaiming that the Church would never give in to Tito's decrees. Lavrenti Beria also must have had complete faith in his own immortality, judging from the crimes of which the ex-chief of the Russian secret police who aspired to succeed Stalin had been accused — including Trotsky's murder — and worse still, "plotting with a foreign power" to overthrow the Soviet regime. His feeling of immortality, however, failed to save him from execution, only nine months after having served as pallbearer to the man of steel. Finally, a third proof of the indestructibility of the feeling of immortality can be gleaned from the fact that Baby M. chose incarnation even after having passed through the nuclear cloud over the atoll of Eniwetok, as she circled the earth. To many, this may seem like sheer innocence; yet, they cannot deny that such innocence has, so far, succeeded in resisting the most powerful mass defect: evidence that the soul itself may be nothing more than a free-floating mass defect, capable of defying probability and putting on or shedding weight as required.

ೞ

Claude takes out the box in which are stored the selection of audio tapes he had integrated into his treatments. This is the first time he has re-examined his collection since leaving Montréal. As he reads the list of titles of these more or less musical experiments, it occurs to him that they provide no new inspiration. He has difficulty even remembering that period of his life, although it was not so long ago. He retrieves the tape entitled *Berlin Woman*, turns the case in his hands, as though it were the fruit of some strange tree.

These days, Claude can't quite make out what is happening to him. He has difficulty following a single train of thought, which actually reflects his errant movements in the physical space of the city. Since arriving in Toronto, Claude has done little else but wander here and there. He has no idea what he is looking for; he's not even sure he is looking for anything. He is simply waiting and watching. Perhaps, one day, something will capture his attention. Nor is he trying to meet someone. He is content to engage in random conversations with people he has no intention of seeing again. His recent encounter with the stranger in the bar marks a break with the anonymity of these last few months. In fact, he wonders what possessed him to give the man his business card. But, as strange as the gesture seems, the realization of this strangeness is fleeting, because already his mind has changed direction, taken another angle, a new tangent. Nothing lasts very long. Each street corner brings a new transformation. But silently. Or almost. As though these were rough sketches, compositions. Attempts, feebly, to lift up his voice. Because finding love does not always depend on the person seeking it. As a matter of fact, Claude does not realize he is thinking of love. He does not realize that love can be a kind of drifting. A vagueness of the soul. A desire seeking itself. Seeking us.

∽

The movies were doing their part, in 1953, to prevent the destruction of the sense of immortality. Their characters swelled the general ranks of humanity and, in populating the earth with more souls than bodies, increased its capacity to counter the mass defect. When you consider that, in 1953, some seven hundred movies shown in theatres in Moncton, Shediac, Bouctouche, and Richibouctou had implanted thousands of characters in the minds of the people of just this small corner of New Brunswick, there is no doubt that, on a global scale, the cinema represented a tremendous force. Nurse Vautour, herself a strong and righteous woman, did not deny herself the pleasure of believing in these characters, in their joys and hardships, and in adopting their attitudes. And, though she sometimes found the Church's reservations exaggerated, she understood that the Church had much to lose in this new game of being. Competition was intense and Jesus Christ, the Church's own main character, was in danger of being upstaged.

Nurse Vautour nevertheless took note that the Church knew a good film when it saw one. For example, The Catholic Cinema Centre found that *The Sound Barrier* (David Lean, 1952) offered "a lesson in courage and professional conscience," though it called on educators to explain the young woman's pregnancy to children. The Centre noted also that "the law of confidentiality to which priests are bound was well portrayed" in *I Confess* (Alfred Hitchcock, 1953), a psycho-religious drama filmed in Québec, starring Montgomery Clift and Anne Baxter. On the other hand, Nurse Vautour did not know what to think of the fact that the Church endorsed Hitchcock's unique talent to "hold an audience in doubt and uncertainty." She was, however, happy to see that, aside from its usual reservations regarding the sexual scenes, the Church generally approved of *Come Back, Little Sheba* (Daniel Mann, 1952), a family drama starring Burt Lancaster and Shirley Booth, who won the prize for best actress both at the Oscars and at Cannes. Nurse Vautour felt the Church's attitude towards the "spinster" played by Katherine Hepburn in *The African Queen* (John Huston, 1951) was rather mean. The Centre did not approve of this prim and proper lady falling suddenly in love with her companion, played by

Humphrey Bogart. Nurse Vautour also felt the Centre was being overly cautious in not recommending this film for children, when it offered "fine moral lessons in duty, courage, endurance, and the influence of education on character." Nurse Vautour had not seen *High Noon* (Fred Zimmermann, 1952), but her brother had, and enjoyed it very much. The Church found some merit in this film, particularly the presentation of "a main character who overcomes his fear to do his duty," but as might have been expected, the religious authorities were not happy about "the discreet allusion to the sheriff's past relationship with a woman in the town." Both the Church and Nurse Vautour enjoyed *Detective Story* (William Wyler, 1951), which painted a picture of a typical afternoon in a New York police station. But the Catholic Centre nevertheless concluded that this "great work containing absolutely moral images" was not appropriate for children. *Moulin Rouge* (John Huston, 1952), starring José Ferrer as the painter Toulouse-Lautrec (he played the entire movie on his knees, with his legs tied behind his back), was roundly condemned: "Toulouse-Lautrec's numerous affairs, the degeneration of this genius into alcohol and lowly passions," required "serious reservations, in spite of the incontestable artistic merit of the film." Probably because of its French title, the film was shown in almost every theatre in French-speaking New Brunswick.

☙

And the ball returns.

No matter how hard she tries, how many loose ends she gathers up, Brigitte can't get past this point. Something sticks to her, something like that ball she keeps sending over, and which keeps returning. Or something like this present that keeps repeating itself, and on which she must nevertheless rely. Brigitte can't quite grasp how it is that she finds herself ensnared in this game. In fact, she does not even know what the game is. She has no clear idea what is going on. Like those neighbourhood kids she once mesmerized, she does not know whether she is on the verge of a higher state of consciousness or simply of losing consciousness. The explosion that has paralyzed her has also revealed a dimension within time, something like an implosion which freezes her to the spot even as it propels her into a great leap forward. Nothing remains as it was. Not even the words. Which she would like to say. To Élizabeth. But which don't seem to come. Won't come.

And yet, there is nothing in what Élizabeth has just told her that surprises or shocks Brigitte. Her silence is neither a reaction nor a response to the postmodern delinquencies evoked by her friend. If we can speak of delinquencies. Words are treacherous. Pregnancies too. One becomes pregnant or contracts AIDS. Life or death. Or both. Or, worst luck: neither. No, having broken with pathologies of all kinds, none of this upsets Brigitte. Yet, clearly, something has caught up with her, something that was seeking her specifically, something like desire, which no one could have suspected, was behind this incredible fragmentation. So that, electrified by destiny which is fulfilled even as it is revealed, Brigitte can do nothing but let this moment be. The nuclear instant exists, of that she is now absolutely certain. And after it comes something which is not quite life and not quite death. Neither is it some kind of sacrifice. Jesus Christ is certainly dead. And has been replaced.

But the ball wants to return. And each ball is a challenge.

8

The Long Road Back

An easy birth — Doses of vitamins and minerals — Waiting for the revelation of the minutely indivisible and the elusively omnipresent — Structure of idleness and verticality of anonymity — Hat sale at Creaghan's — Boredom as a sign which does not lie — Entanglement of freedom and the mystery of origins — Time as a virtue — Surrender and the point of no return — A moment of human warmth — Multiple layers of solidarity — The Flemming's salad — Internal arrangement and the play of mirrors — Instant of desire and the ball which keeps coming back

IN THE END, Baby M. met her deadline of November 1953 and slipped into life with all her parts and a few tears, for which she earned a paragraph in *l'Évangéline*. She was, however, hiding a congenital metabolic anomaly, which took the form of slight digestive problems during the first days of her extra-uterine existence. But the digestive problems soon disappeared and the disease remained in a latent state for several months. It then resurfaced as a case of bronchitis, but this rather common condition passed without raising any celiac suspicions. A precise diagnosis was only made in July 1954, when the disease finally exhausted its disguises and drastic measures were required to check the profuse and nauseating diarrhea with which Baby M.'s mother, helpless at the sight of her child wasting away, could no longer cope.

The sight of the child's body, which had begun to wither and showed the early signs of malnutrition, sent a kind of shock wave through Moncton's Hôtel-Dieu l'Assomption. No matter whether the source of the illness was attributed to an infection of the respiratory canal or to some sort of emotional or psychological problem, the case was rare. Baby M., for her part, did not realize that her little game would shake the very raison d'être of the hospital, whose mission was also the survival of the Acadian people. Already entirely preoccupied by the effect of "Nature" on her "style," Baby M. had no idea how big a fuss she was causing, just as she had no way of appreciating her pediatrician's acumen, the warmth of Nurse Vautour's embrace, or the discipline of the kitchen staff, which were absolutely forbidden to serve her anything but banana, liver, or chicken purée. At one point, the kitchen was authorized to deviate slightly from this routine and to prepare an egg purée but, following Baby M.'s highly unfavourable reaction to the new dish, this happy occasion was never repeated. As for the other nutrients essential to the child's growth, they would be provided by proteined milk and doses of vitamins and minerals.

જી

Claude did his best, in the short time available, to set up the room in his Toronto apartment where he would give massages. When he first arrived in the city, he had been unsure whether he wanted to take up the profession again, and so had merely stored his equipment in the room where, should he ever decide to do so, he could exercise his practice. As he shut the door to the room, he had sensed the gesture might be final. This was, by no means, the first period of freedom he had allowed himself. All his life, Claude had been careful not to go forward blindly, maintaining for himself and in himself a space where something new might arise, the sort of thing that comes as long as we reach out to it, that takes shape without ever being nameable or definite. Because in the continuum that extends between what is minutely indivisible and what is elusively omnipresent, something new is always taking shape.

It was this unknowable side of life that Claude was addressing when he prepared the room where he would receive the stranger from the bar, to whom he implicitly offered his services. Strange gesture, indeed. Claude does not really know why he offered the invitation. He realized this as he was doing it, as though someone else were acting through him. In any case, and even though he senses this first session will also be the last, Claude will put his whole heart into it. Having always done his work seriously, he could not bear to perform his final act in a half-finished place, in a room where idleness was already apparent. He has, therefore, done his best to make the room impeccable, as though it had always existed, would always exist. Because, in fact, as Claude well knows, it does exist forever in the mind of the customer who comes.

გ

Because of the congenital nature of celiac disease, it is highly unlikely that the events which marked the end of 1953 and the beginning of 1954 had more than a minor effect on Baby M. The importance of the events that spanned her hospital stay in July 1954 is also difficult to measure. Aside from the agreement that put an end to the Trieste conflict, *l'Évangéline* had covered the talks aimed at reestablishing peace in Indochina and the continuing nuclear tests by the Americans in the Bikini and Eniwetok islands. The Acadian daily also reported the euphoria in Great Britain, following the end of meat rationing, which dated back to the start of the Second World War. The ghost of that war continued to haunt people's minds, if only because the conflict had allowed the Communists to demonstrate their determination. In Great Britain, Winston Churchill continued to preach a hard line against the Reds, and he made certain that Great Britain joined the United States in opposing the admission of Red China to the United Nations. A few countries, including India and New Zealand, denounced this opposition, and a large number of North Americans agreed. These North Americans were beginning to feel that "anti-Communist paranoia and McCarthyist stupidity" had gone on long enough.

As far as the Moncton region was concerned, there was not much, in 1954, to get excited about. Were it not for the sales on hats at Creaghan's (all prices had been cut, even those of white hats) and dresses, coats, and suits at Peake's, things would have been at a complete standstill. One had to look to Shediac to find a more exciting event: the Lobster Festival. A little further, in Percé, a soon-to-be famous trial was beginning: a prospector named Coffin had been accused of killing three Americans on a bear hunt in the

Gaspé. The discovery of the three bodies, in July 1953, had made the top ten list of the year's events in Canada. The news that the celebrated Dionne quintuplets would once again be reunited also caused a stir. A bit bony but smiling, after her nine months with the Servantes du Très Saint-Sacrement of Québec, Marie Dionne explained that boredom and loss of appetite had forced her to leave the cloister. She was going home for the summer, to rest and reflect on her future. She would not rule out a return to the nuns, but her comment, "it was awfully boring," left little doubt in anyone's mind as to the outcome.

₰

Still seated in her friend Brigitte's office, Élizabeth senses that this silence has lasted long enough and something must now happen. She feels she has reached the end of this particular mental state. There is nothing more to be gained or learned from it, at least for the moment. This impossibility of going any further reminds her of the sea, when it withdraws to its furthest point from the coast, leaving large expanses of bare wet sand behind. Élizabeth can feel the sensation of the hard, damp sand beneath her feet. She can see the sea in the distance, having filled its lungs in one long deep breath, now preparing to return to the shore. With a kind of languor. And some hesitation. Advancing and retreating. But, slyly, each time advancing a little more than it retreats. As though it were trying to outwit something, something too predictable perhaps.

Suddenly Élizabeth feels fine. As though she were relaxing at the thought of herself there, on the damp sand, watching the sea come in. Suddenly it is as though her whole life had been a long preparation for some inevitable return. She breathes, replenishing herself by watching the sea and sensing, at her side, all those who, like her, wait by the edge for the indomitable to return and take its place in the contour of the shoreline. Because the entire coast seems always to be turned towards this eternal return, as though all of our lives were but a long preparation for an encounter. Evidence of something to come. As certainly as cliffs rise up at the water's edge. A proof that the future, though it remains hidden from us, is predestined.

And so, Élizabeth's road back to Moncton, and to the sea. To a kind of end of the earth, but where she feels reborn. And somehow more definite this time. More conscious. To the point that even her name seems less strange to her now. *Élizabeth.* The entanglement of being, in the image of that Acadian entanglement, rolling along free and easy, and which one can only admire as it passes. Like a vagabond on the road. Heading towards his next destination. Which may turn out to be a detour. A detour which, in the end, does not matter, since he carries his roots with him. Which one can always try to untangle from the rest. If one is so inclined. An often tedious enterprise. Attributable to the novel. If the novel could. Or an illness. Whether major or common. Or a mystery. The mystery of origins. Which every life must probe.

❧

Neither distant events nor intensive care seemed to have any effect on Baby M.'s health in the days which followed her admission to the hospital. The child continued her day-to-day peristaltic routine, oblivious to all, and assailing the olfactory sensibilities of any who ventured near. In fact, aside from her intestinal battles which certainly tired her out, Baby M. seemed content to whimper from time to time, to sleep and eat, to be washed and cared for like a real baby. She manifested no inclination and seemed to make no effort to get better. Those who followed her progress closely could easily see there was nothing to do but wait. No one could guess what would cause a breakthrough, but there could be no doubt it would have to come with time.

Time, therefore, had become the main ally of the doctor, Nurse Vautour, the committed scriptor father, and the queen and martyr mother. Each recognized time as absolute master of the situation, taking precedence over all other considerations and intentions, good or bad. Each dedicated her or himself to this belief, as to a virtue, patiently and without expecting anything in return. If the reward came, so be it. Baby M.'s life, whatever its length, would be complete. It occupied its rightful place in the consciousness of minds and bodies. No other prayer was possible. Nothing more could be done. There was no system upon which to rely. Nothing but resignation. Total resignation to events as they would unfold. It was not even something one could experience as waiting. It had to be experienced in the present, because only the present can sustain and inscribe life for all time.

Which finally came to pass after thirteen days. But those thirteen days without any noticeable change, that endless wandering punctuated by counter-currents, each seemingly as determining as the other, in short this completely nebulous existence was cause for great concern for the future health of the child. For medical science had already noted that celiac children tended to become hypochondriacs. As for Nurse Vautour, her suspicions were elsewhere. She was afraid the child would take a liking to this delirium; would begin to take some pleasure in allowing her spirit to float above her body, even allowing it to drift each time a little farther, just to see how far the soul could travel from the body. She could sense, all around Baby M., a kind of celiac zone, in which the soul could actually survive without the body. Something like the way movie characters can live without flesh and bones. Nurse Vautour feared that Baby M. would venture too far and, without realizing it, cross the threshold through which there is no coming back. The child seemed to her brave but somewhat reckless to take such risks. Such were her thoughts, more or less, as she swaddled the child and rocked her, before placing her back in her crib. She rocked Baby M. gently and silently, just in case simple human warmth might make a difference.

∾

Claude opens the door to the man he believes will be his last client. And, for once, he is more conscious of his own embarrassment than the customer's. But this shyness will not take root, thanks to the natural calm of the stranger from the bar. By the time he has begun to explain his method of work, Claude has already regained his confidence. Leading the way to the massage room, he explains that his treatments are in no way sexual, but that the massage often provokes an erection in male clients, who should not be surprised. As Claude is about to leave the room while his client undresses, the stranger from the bar suddenly extends a hand and introduces himself. Claude realizes that, until this moment, he had been avoiding introducing himself. In fact, he rarely introduces himself. Doing so always makes him feel as though he has lost his verticality, melted and been spread thin, become diffuse. He has always felt taller and straighter in anonymity. But, faced with the extended hand of the stranger from the bar, he introduces himself anyway, since there is always the possibility that this time things will be different.

Claude has no difficulty relating to this new body. Quickly, he re-establishes contact with that particular feeling, both essential and distant, that dwells in the elasticity, smooth-ness, and warmth of skin. Moving to and fro in the long tranquil memory that wants only to go on forever, he rediscovers the precision and understanding in his hands. He had forgotten that they have a life and intelligence of their own. He had forgotten, too, that this profession has a way of bringing out the best in him, his knowledge and sensitivity merging into a fundamental certainty, the cer-tainty of the body. To the point that he loses all sense of time. Already, the moment has come to ask his client to turn over onto his back. As always, he is careful not to lose contact with the client's body while the latter undertakes this movement.

At the outset of a treatment, Claude always makes sure to keep a hand on the client's body in order not to break the thread of the contact. But as a session progresses, his sense of touch grows stronger and the contact zone extends beyond the body to the surrounding space. The slightest gesture becomes an expression of personality, the masseur's as well as the client's. In this sense, the client's way of turning represents to Claude a crucial movement, at once an indication, a critical point, and a kind of sexual moment.

For Claude cannot help but read the soul's features on the chest as it is exposed, more or less timidly, in a gesture of surrender and confidence. And, as the client turns over, his contact with Claude hangs by nothing more than a slight brushing of the hand, accompanying the movement with infinite subtlety, with a pivotal gaze, like a dancer encircling his ballerina.

Claude's last client turns over rather gracefully on the narrow table, and now the masseur's hands advance, in a series of successive surprises, over the multiple layers of the chest, each of them solid but without the slightest rigidity, without hardness. Claude's hands could wander here forever. As in sand. They would even like to slide beneath the skin to feel this materiality from within. Warm. Enveloping. Then, lost in a reverie of sensations, Claude brushes, quite by accident, the man's awakened sex. He is returned to reality; gradually abandons the client's chest to continue the treatment elsewhere. As he watches his hands work, more and more feeling their breath as he moves forward, Claude regains his confidence before the miracle of the body and the spirit. At the end, to keep the client from catching cold, Claude lays a light silk sheet over him. Then, so as to preserve something of all this, to preserve something of the miracle, he lays his hand on the man's sex, pressing down a little, for several moments, before leaving.

❧

At first, Nurse Vautour thought it was a mirage: Baby M. playing in her bed. After thirteen days of what felt like crossing a desert, Nurse Vautour was not quite ready to trust her eyes. She did not want to mistake a mere gesture or accidental gurgle for a playful spirit. So she hung back for a few minutes and observed Baby M. She was not wrong. Baby M. was truly lively. Her eyes were wide open and she was happily moving her head and arms. She was even amusing herself by making sounds. Still not willing to believe too quickly in this transformation, Nurse Vautour withheld any expression of her joy. And she was glad of her prudent reserve when, two days later, Baby M. relapsed into full intestinal hyperactivity and even more-than-usual crying. However, already somehow conscious of the power and fragility of signs, Baby M. did not wait long before rekindling her nurse's hopes. A few days later, she feigned interest in the bars of her bed. Excellent strategy, because two days later, Nurse Vautour offered up a special prayer for Baby M. during mass on Vocation Sunday.

Though she was convinced Baby M. was saved, Nurse Vautour was careful to conceal this in her presence since she was a writer's daughter. It was as though the nurse also understood the power and fragility of signs. Sensing that Baby M. might misinterpret an excess of attention, she remained prudent. The following days seemed to prove her right, because Baby M. once again did her utmost to digest badly, with some success. Nevertheless, Nurse Vautour sensed a lack of conviction. Deep down, she was fairly certain that Baby M. had turned back, and was now on the road to recovery. Still, the nurse predicted it would be a long road. She had not forgotten that Baby M. would have to get used to the totally mundane nature of healthy life, a reality she would also have to learn to digest. Baby M. would also have to learn to accept not knowing where she had come from. She would have to learn to live content, like everyone else, with contemplating her origins from afar. The further along the road to recovery she travelled, the more Baby M. would forget what she was leaving behind. She would therefore also have to get used to the idea of forgetting. Nurse Vautour kept a watchful eye on these various operations of detachment. It took another week before all the elements of the process were coordinated and operational. Everyone — the doctor, the nurse, the committed scriptor father, and the queen and martyr mother — watched and waited for a clear point of change, an irrefutable sign of recovery. Now that there was hope, they were eager to leave the sanctuary of time and deal with the more commonplace things in life apart from this child under the spell of writing a brackish novel. They were almost fed up with being baffled by Baby M.'s global perspective, which gave her a head start of discouragement or delight over other human beings.

When the sign they were all waiting for finally came, naturally, no one missed it, least of all Nurse Vautour. Baby M., who until then had always lain on her back, rolled over onto her side. Nurse Vautour would never forget the sight of the child's tiny curved back, a child who, until that moment, had shown neither the strength nor the desire to change position. Without any help, Baby M. turned over as though she had decided to cuddle up in the palm of life. Naturally, this quarter turn took on the proportions of a major event and sent a second shock wave through l'Hôtel-Dieu l'Assomption. In the kitchens, the employees broke open the cherry jars and garnished everyone's dessert in celebration of the child's recovery. No matter that, on that day, *l'Évangéline* reported a crazy woman had stabbed a priest at the altar, and that work would have to be rationed;

nothing, nothing at all could block the path of Baby M.'s life.

They kept Baby M. in the hospital for several more days, just to firm up her desire to live. Her entrails continued to churn her food all over the place, but the turmoil had lost its significance. From now on they would have to consider her distended abdomen and soft, greasy, nauseating excrement as relatively normal, in the hope that this rather strange behaviour would vanish gradually over time. Retrieving her child from the arms of Nurse Vautour, Baby M.'s mother may not have realized all she was in for, but she felt prepared. The doctor had explained that Baby M.'s particularity could last for many years before expressing itself in a cleaner manner. Baby M.'s mother savoured a first momentary respite after supper when, fed and washed, the child fell quietly asleep in her crib in the corner of the kitchen. Meanwhile, in a rocking chair nearby, her soul at peace, her mother perused *l'Évangéline*, stopping for a moment on the detail of a salad that Mrs. Hugh John Flemming had prepared for her husband, the premier of New Brunswick. The paper had published the article to mark Salad Week. Further along, she read that one day the sea would feed the entire earth, and that farmers' children would eventually grow old, like everyone else. This set her thinking about her own children, who would revel, the next day, in their father's presence — barring some unforeseen journalistic event, of course. The eldest of the five, who had recently learned to operate the radio, had just turned it on and the voice of Luis Mariano filled the room with an exotic mood resembling hope.

❧

Sitting across from her friend Brigitte, Élizabeth cannot speak of the peaceful images and sensations which have infiltrated her being. She feels incapable of manipulating the words so as to pass them unbroken through the enormous wall of concrete that surrounds her friend and herself. And yet, something strains to break through this incommunicativeness. Some tiny something that is still communicative, and that might slice through the thickness of this moment and set life going again. But, unable to work it out clearly, Élizabeth resigns herself to telling her friend that she is going to have her hair cut before starting back for Moncton. This declaration almost startles Brigitte. She is astonished by the offhand manner of her friend, who has always resisted any change to her hairdo. Taken aback also by this departure which seems precipitated, Brigitte struggles to understand the haunting impression that something will be left unfinished. She is suddenly aware of a kind of hyper-present, and an imminent rearrangement of sorts. She did not see this rearrangement coming, though it directly concerns her, completely disrupts her internal balance, leaving her caught between feelings of affection and desire. Surprise. Slight skip of the heart over the abyss. A burst of laughter from Brigitte, who cannot restrain this loving laughter at the sight of Élizabeth looking for the hairdresser's number in the phone book. She rises. Takes Élizabeth by the arm and leads her to the closet mirror.

Standing behind Élizabeth as they face the mirror, Brigitte gathers her friend's hair to create the effect of short hair. Élizabeth turns her head to one side and the other, the two of them trying to decide just how much needs to be uncovered. Uncovered. To see in Brigitte's gaze that something which cuts through to the reality of the moment, that something that goes beyond the present, that something that allows Élizabeth and Brigitte to look at each other, to really look at each other. And this look is good. It is clear and honest. It is enough to carry Brigitte's hand, as it caresses, ever so lightly, the side of Élizabeth's face. Then the neck, ever so lightly. And onward, extending, to stretch across, to lie for a moment on her breast, before once again taking up its movement straight down along the sternum. Two women. Not understanding entirely what is being said, but allowing it to be said. Brigitte's hand continuing to follow the straight line, over the stomach, the abdomen, to finally press lightly, ever so lightly, the mound of desire. While their eyes remain locked together. For there is no elsewhere.

And though the ball returns, followed by another, and yet another, Brigitte refuses to be rushed.

Epilogues

The royal family's instinct for self-sacrifice and survival —
Frogmore and Buckingham gardens — Firm extensions of
continuity — Writing versus the inability to communicate —
Optimism or pessimism of Samuel Beckett — Alfred
Nobel and the pure poetic folly — Science and language:
a rereading of radioactivity — The thirteenth train —
Another Marian coincidence in Acadia — Three hundred
days of indulgence and the double waffle-maker — Aerial
perspective of desire — Sooner or later the ball — A
colossal labour of creation — Rereading of the demise of
l'Évangéline and the parable of the reconstructive effort —
The Corfu impulse — Primordial undifferentiation and
the dangers of a distorted image of oneself — The reign of
necessity

THE DUKE OF WINDSOR paid the rest of his
life for dishonouring his family. His dishonour was com-
pounded by the fact that, at the end of the First World War,

the royal family had come to represent all the best qualities of the English race. Such prestige was at least in part attributable to George V, father of the man who would be demoted to the ducal rank. The former's behaviour, "full of good sense and dedication to his duties," had renewed the British subjects' confidence in the Crown. In 1915, for example, as the English were beginning to worry about the effects of alcohol on their nation, George V decreed that his family and the court would abstain from any consumption of alcoholic beverages until the end of the war. This was by no means an inconsequential decision, since it was general knowledge that the king "bore no personal hostility to the bottle." For their part, his subjects continued to drink as before, but "they appreciated their monarch's sacrifice all the more for being able to measure its magnitude." Two years later, when ties to Germany, no matter how slight, became particularly unseemly, George V decided to change the name of his dynasty from *Hanover* to the typically English *Windsor*, and suggested that "those of his cousins who bore a Germanic patronymic exchange it for an English-sounding one." These measures, along with the fact that the royal couple's eldest sons "wore the uniform and were occasionally exposed to the risk of being hit by shell fragments," propelled the royal family into the hearts of the entire nation. But there was a price to pay for this favoured status. The royal family was obliged, in a sense, to be virtuous in place of the English people themselves, who had begun to take pleasure in a degree of moral freedom. Strengthened by the love of his treasured Wallis, Edward VIII refused to comply with this game of purity by proxy. As a consequence, he lived his entire life burdened by his family's disapproval. Even Elizabeth II, in spite of all her qualities, did not seem prepared to forget the past and establish openly cordial relations with her uncle the duke and his wife the duchess.

Nevertheless, in 1960, following some delicate negotiations, the queen agreed to one of the duke's requests: to be buried, when the time came, with his wife, in the gardens of Frogmore, which he adored. In 1964, the queen sent flowers to her uncle, who had undergone heart surgery in a Texas hospital. Three months later, after the duke's eye operation in a London clinic, the queen sent him some foie gras, and then visited him herself. Here, Elizabeth II saw the Duchess of Windsor again for the first time since 1936. In the heat of the moment, the queen went so far as to authorize the duke to walk in Buckingham gardens, in the company of his valet, during his convalescence. Finally, three years later, in 1967, one of the duke's fondest wishes was granted, a wish the duke had expressed in 1940, several years after his marriage to Mrs. Simpson. In the hope that an official royal audience would put an end to all the tongue-wagging and ugly rumours concerning the duchess, the dethroned king had asked the petrified royal family to receive his wife were it only for fifteen minutes. And so it was that, four days after their thirtieth wedding anniversary, the duke and duchess participated, for the first time, in a royal ceremony as husband and wife. The couple were permitted to take their place in the front row, beside Queen Elizabeth, her husband Prince Philip, and the Queen Mother. The ceremony — the unveiling of a commemorative plaque in honour of Queen Mary — lasted exactly fifteen minutes.

According to the biographer Michael Bloch, no other such invitation was ever extended to the Windsors, not even when the duke's health failed in 1972. That winter, the duke's illness caused great concern for British diplomats stationed in Paris, home of the duke and duchess. The diplomats had been instructed to make sure the disgraced uncle should not die during Elizabeth II's upcoming official visit to Paris. British officials feared that the duke's death at that moment might hinder the queen's crucial mission, involving negotiations on the projected creation of the European Economic Community. The British ambassador in Paris went so far as to visit the duke's doctor to inform him that it would be acceptable for the duke to die before or after the visit, but not during. In the end, the duke survived the queen's visit; she even came to see him. Though extremely ill, the duke refused to receive his niece in his pyjamas in bed. The nursing staff helped him to dress appropriately and to sit in a chair in a sitting room adjacent to his bedroom. The intravenous tubes were concealed beneath his clothes, and the intravenous pole was hidden by a curtain behind his chair. The nursing staff watched, transfixed in fear, as the duke, in spite of his weakness, rose to salute his queen on her arrival. No such movement having been planned, the caregivers were afraid the entire trompe-l'oeil installation would collapse. Their fears were unjustified, as all the extensions held firm. The visit lasted a quarter of an hour. The duke's health declined rapidly in the days that followed and the cancer carried him off ten days after he had greeted his niece Elizabeth, whom he had never ceased to recognize as his sovereign. Thus are the paths of continuity entirely hidden to us.

℘

Much could be said regarding Élizabeth's inability to communicate to her friend Brigitte the essence of the images flashing across her mind during the silence which preceded their scene before the mirror. At first glance, it might be tempting to attribute this inability to communicate to a degree of laziness on the novelist's part. But a look back at the year 1953 provides a far more nuanced view. Because it was in 1953, as Winston Churchill was being recognized with a Nobel Prize for his qualities as a man of letters and for his rousing speeches on freedom and human dignity, a year, therefore, of wind and speech, that Samuel Beckett published *The Unnamable*. This writer who would end up describing "a large idiotic mouth . . . that speaks in vain" would also be Nobelized, but not until 1969, and not without a heated debate within the Nobel Committee. The argument ranged over the entire gamut of issues, from Alfred Nobel's initial intention to the true import of literature. The process leading to recognition of Beckett's work constituted a turning point for the Swedish Academy of Letters, resulting in important changes in the way the academy would thereafter consider literary works.

The divisions which became public with the awarding of the Nobel Prize in literature to Mr. Beckett had already been germinating in the guise of a malaise at the time of Churchill's Nobelization. To put it briefly, after Churchill, the Swedish Academy never rewarded another writer who was essentially a historian, nor an elected representative occupying public office, which disadvantaged André Malraux and Léopold Senghor. But these decisions only partially reflected the dilemma faced by the Nobel Committee for literature after the war, a dilemma that resulted in its oscillating between recognition of the works of masters on the one hand, and that of innovators on the other. The masters were recognized for their power and intensity

(Russell in 1950, Lagerkvist in 1951, Mauriac in 1952, Churchill in 1953); the innovators for their audacity, resulting in the renewal of language, style, and form (Hesse in 1946, Gide in 1947, Eliot in 1948, Faulkner in 1949). Overall, the innovators dominated the period after the war, that is from 1946 to 1960. In 1954, Hemingway was judged to be both a master and an innovator, Laxness in 1955 and Jiménez in 1956 were innovators, as was Pasternak in 1958, Quasimodo in 1959, and St.-John Perse in 1960. Camus's place in this portrait is difficult to fix. Nobelized in 1957, he was a writer of his time who was recognized as such.

The recognition of innovators lost some ground during the sixties. According to Kjell Espmark, historian of the Nobel Prize in literature, this loss of ground is related to the very nature of innovation, which, once it is initiated, never lasts long. Thus, Neruda (1971), Martinson (1974), and Milosz (1980) "do not belong to the heroic period of modernism but rather to the period in which it collects its laurels." As for Beckett, although he was an innovator, his work required some innovation in the very criteria of innovation. Basically, the question was whether Beckett was an optimist or a pessimist and, consequently, if his work could be considered as *idealistic*, according to Alfred Nobel's stipulation. In the end, it was demonstrated that the notion of idealism included that of integrity and, on that score, though "situated in the general neighbourhood of nothingness," Beckett's work "contains a love for humanity which is increasingly marked by understanding as it descends into abjection." Another of Beckett's defenders argued that "by an effect of sheer contrast, the myth of annihilation so dear to Beckett is coloured by the myth of creation," which has the result of making nothingness "somehow liberating and stimulating."

After Beckett's Nobelization, the optimistic or pessimistic nature of a literary work was never again a serious factor, and by the time Claude Simon's work underwent Nobel scrutiny, in 1985, little attention was given to his "obsession with violence and brutal domination." The jurists, recognizing in him one of the leaders of the French *nouveau roman*, concluded that he had enriched the epic art "with a dense and suggestive canvas of words, events, and places, including slippages and juxtapositions of elements according to a logic other than that imposed by the realist continuity of time and space." In any case, in the interval between the Nobelization of Simon and that of Beckett, the members of the Nobel Committee of the Swedish Academy of Letters had taken a pragmatic turn in their pursuit of innovation. Armed with terms like "prolific," "productive," and "promising," they no longer hesitated to bring pioneers out of the shadows and into the international spotlight, having decided that the literary award of awards should serve those who write as much as those who read.

&

As important as the Nobel Prize in literature is, most writers, having no hope of winning it, easily console themselves with the knowledge that their true reward is in the poetry itself. The impulse to write springs from an inexplicable hope, which makes life the fruit of a poetic folly as pure as Alfred Nobel's testament. Just as Mr. Nobel's will demonstrated the importance attributed to that which is written down, inscribed for all time, so all writing includes something of the testament. It perpetuates all of life into a great beyond occasionally open to speech, but upon which only writing can build. Thus, the writer, through his work, aims not at wrapping himself in the banality of personal immortality, but rather to become part of a force that moves, in a kind of current or tidal bore — why not! — stirring the fish and the algae for the benefit of the shore birds, who catch them on the fly, for they too are in a hurry to counter the mass defect. The mass defect. Something like a soul without strings, completely free to navigate the heights, in marvellous and supernatural flight, up where origins and meaning have no hold.

Alfred Nobel's will did more than confirm the aura of writing. Because he was a genius with the means to exercise his genius, Mr. Nobel was able to celebrate the marriage of science and language. For science and poetry have always drawn from the same words to speak to each other, creating together the foundations of the real, at times virtually eliminating the gap between the language of science and the science of language. Like Élizabeth and Brigitte when their trajectories intersect. For that matter, the entire phenomenon of radioactivity is rarely if ever discussed in terms of the small poetic marvel that it is. In a world that swears by the hard work of knowledge, perhaps we should remember that the nuclei of certain atoms emit rays spontaneously, and that the principle characteristic of spontaneity is that it produces itself without constraint. There are also lessons to be learned from the power of these spontaneous emissions. About alpha rays, for example, we should know that they can be blocked by a few centimetres of air or a sheet of paper. A sheet of paper, so once again poetry! Beta rays, on the other hand, can travel through a metal plate several millimetres thick. Clearly, they are real go-getters. With or without a Nobel Prize, they work hard all their lives to make their way, to break through barriers. Because, in the scientific world, as in the world of language, it's all a matter of barriers, of forging ahead. As for gamma rays, similar in nature to X rays, we might as well say that nothing can stop them, not even tens of centimetres of concrete. Unstoppable, they rapidly become absolutes themselves and new barriers for others to break through. Finally, the fact that these spontaneous emissions can be detrimental to the human body demonstrates that humanity is always vulnerable. In that sense, the impulse to write may in fact be a weapon, a defensive reflex, a spontaneous emission directed at the unfathomable, at once breath and breadth, desire for poetry, and poetry of desire.

છ

According to *l'Évangéline*, the American singer Hank Williams died the first day of January 1953, struck down by a heart attack in Oak Hill, Virginia, en route to Ohio, where he was scheduled to give a concert. At the end of the same month, the Russians lost their twenty-five-year-old caviar concession in the Iranian waters of the Caspian Sea, as Iran decided to take up the lucrative commerce itself rather than renew the agreement. In the spring, Jackie Robinson, the first black man to be admitted into major league baseball, announced his retirement. Several days later, jazzmen Tommy and Jimmy Dorsey reunited after a twenty-year feud. In Canada, farmers were preparing to sow twenty-six million acres of wheat and nine million acres of barley. This would yield a harvest of six hundred million bushels of wheat in the Prairies, the second largest in the country's history. At the end of 1953, Canada was crowned producer of the best wheat of the year for the twenty-fifth time in the thirty years the contest had been held. Unfortunately, nothing could be worse for a celiac child than the gluten present in wheat and other cereals. But it was not gluten that stirred the entrails of Baby M.'s parents and Nurse Vautour that spring. In Louisiana, where a major branch of the Acadian tree flourished, bus drivers had launched a strike against a new by-law allowing blacks to sit in the front of the bus when the rear seats were all occupied.

The people of the Atlantic coast watched with similar astonishment mixed with incomprehension the conflict caused by the presence of a Russian religious sect, the Doukhobors, in the Kootenay and Okanagan valleys of British Columbia. These "sons of freedom" were suspected of having set more than twenty fires and planning to dynamite train bridges and other rail lines of the Canadian Pacific in the area. The authorities had imprisoned the 150 members of the sect who had paraded nude in front of the school in Perry Siding, where the government had consigned their children. For some reason, the Doukhobors did not want their children in school. They began a hunger strike in prison. On the sixth day of their fast, they had not yet received "the word of God to end the strike." On the eighth day, they asked for fruit. Without saying whether the Doukhobors had received their divine message in the interim, *l'Évangéline* moved on to the discovery of the source of the Amazon, the turbulent Apurimac River, and to the global vagabond, Michael Patrick O'Brien, who had finally found asylum in the Dominican Republic. The ex-barman from Shanghai had lived on cargo ships and travelled the oceans for three years because no country would accept him.

The meaning of all this? The Englishman George Lesley best summarized the situation as he lay in a Dartford hospital with a leg fracture and other injuries "after lying on the tracks, unable to move, while twelve trains ran over him." Lesley, who had not lost consciousness during the entire ordeal, said he was grateful there had been no thirteenth train, because he was sure it would have been unlucky for him.

∾

For Acadians, accustomed to Marian coincidences, 1953 could not have ended on a better note than with the proclamation, by the pope himself, of the Marian Year. Indeed, thanks to this announcement, it was as though the year were not ending at all. It would slide instead into a long slow crescendo, beginning on the night of December 7 to 8, and ending exactly one year later on December 8, 1954, the one hundredth anniversary of the declaration by Pope Pius IX of the dogma of the Immaculate Conception of the Mother of God. In that memorable year, the infallible pontiff had declared that "the doctrine according to which the Blessed Virgin Mary had been, from the first moment of her conception, by the grace and singular privilege of all-powerful God, and in anticipation of the merits of Jesus Christ, Saviour of humanity, preserved and exempted from all trace of original sin, is a doctrine revealed by God and which, therefore, must be firmly and inviolably believed by all the faithful." To mark the inauguration of this "small Holy Year," a mass would be celebrated at half-past midnight in a number of parishes, and the faithful who had not eaten since midnight could take communion, on the condition they pray for the intentions decreed by the Holy Father during at least two hours previous (a period which could include the duration of the mass). These intentions were addressed first to young people, "that they apply themselves in mortifying their passions, practising purity, and resisting corruption through worldliness," then to the elderly, "that they distinguish themselves by their honesty, fidelity to the domestic hearth, and the care they give to raising their children properly." They were also addressed to the Mother of God, asking her to intervene so that the hungry, the oppressed, and refugees be granted justice, peace, and a homeland. People prayed also for the freedom of the Church, "that God, by the intercession of Mary, break the bonds upon freedom of conscience," and that He give imprisoned or exiled priests "the joy of returning to their flocks." Finally, they prayed for the coming of peace, under the patronage of the Blessed Virgin who gave the world the Prince of Peace. The inauguration of the Marian Year continued during the day of December 8, 1953, in Rome, where a half-million people lined up to see his Holiness Pius XII travel the four miles between the Roman basilicas of St. Peter and St. Mary Maggiore. As had been prearranged, when the pope's car arrived at St. Mary Maggiore's, women waved handkerchiefs to commemorate the snowfall by which the Virgin Mary had identified the spot upon which to build the basilica.

In the Acadian archdiocese, where the hundredth anniversary of the dogma of the Immaculate Conception coincided with the fiftieth anniversary of the crowning of the national Madonna, the invitation to celebrate the Marian Year took on the force of a command. A pastoral letter, delivered to all leaders of the faith, listed various ways of celebrating

Mary's glory: by raising a Marian sanctuary in an easily accessible spot in every church; by establishing Marian sanctuaries in every family; by giving conferences, sermons, and instructions on Marian devotions; by the daily recitation of the rosary in every family; by making monthly preparatory novenas and reciting the Litanies of Loreto on the first Saturday of every month; by reciting the prayer of the Marian Year every Sunday and statutory holiday during the year; by renewing, in October, the oaths of the Crusade of the Rosary; and finally, by the participation of students in Marian competitions and meetings, in writing essays, making scrapbooks and albums. The pastoral letter also offered priests a selection of appropriate sermons, invited them to participate in Marian days and pilgrimages, and urged them to foster a Marian atmosphere in their parishes and dioceses. They were also asked to inform the faithful of the program of indulgences for the Marian Year, including the invocation "O Mary conceived without sin, pray for us who beseech you," which alone was worth three hundred days of indulgence. The greater part of the letter was published in *l'Évangéline* on December 7, 1953. An advertisement for Moncton Plumbing took up the rest of the page. It suggested that readers electrify their lives with modern miracles by buying, for Christmas, a Westinghouse refrigerator or washing machine, or an iron, toaster, or double waffle-maker.

∽

Back in her office after having walked Élizabeth to the elevator, Brigitte stands before the large window, watching the movement of passers-by on the street below. She is waiting for the appearance of Élizabeth, who, any moment now, will slip back into the turbulence of life. She thinks she knows what direction her friend will take. She can already imagine her stride and long coat. She also senses her characteristic pale melancholy, a mood Brigitte rarely experiences, being generally swept up in the play of discovery. Then she remembers that old scene from her childhood. Once again she is on the high seas, personifying love. She can see the astonished faces of the neighbourhood children, who seemed so perfectly to understand the drama of love and solitude. As though they could also understand the way something can be huge and yet escape us, or escape us for the moment but become one with eternity. And for an instant, Brigitte grasps once again the simultaneously dual nature of every experience. Permanence and impermanence. Something played out and something passed on. Something passed on and something which nevertheless continues on its way forever. Each person's DNA and destiny, its appointed hour, its moment of truth.

Torn between a general feeling of magnitude and the sense that every human life hangs by a single thread, Brigitte finally spots Élizabeth emerging from the shadow of the buildings. It is as though she were emerging from the entrails of the earth. She follows her, watches her back as she moves up that most romantic of avenues. She knows the autumn light on her face. She hears music, envisions a film, senses a story, maybe even History, in this projection on the border between reality and the imaginary. Then Élizabeth disappears onto a side street. Brigitte is left with a feeling both peaceful and disquieting. Unsure of what to return to, she looks down to the other end of the court. Something hesitates. And yet, she can see the ball. It is bouncing around, but not in her direction. As though the ball had begun to play its own game. Brigitte watches. Waits. Will continue to wait. For the ball to decide. For the ball to return.

Because each ball is a challenge.

დ

Recalling the relentless labour required to publish the daily *Évangéline* during the fifties, Baby M.'s father would later admit that nothing seemed less certain than the paper's survival. Because any one of several factors could cripple the enterprise, Baby M.'s father knew that disaster was only as far away as a bit of "bad luck, a slip, or merely the combination, according to the law of possibilities, of any two of those factors." The dedicated scriptor and his colleagues toiled mainly just to put off that fateful day. And though the composition of the team changed over time, the publication of *l'Évangéline* was always an adventure, an adventure that lasted from September 1949 to September 1982.

Naturally, the working conditions of these "pioneer labourers" were modest: antiquated typewriters and salaries, and virtually endless days. The hindsight provided by Saturdays off only made Sundays all the more unbearable. On that day, the enterprise was like a monster they would never slay. Baby M.'s father remembers once "crossing his arms on a pile of papers on his desk, dropping his head, and crying like a baby." Seeing this, a fellow worker had been moved, but refrained from intervening. Two hours later, the energy had returned to the editorial offices, where all incoming stories were in English. No one here was above translation, or working the humble parish life, sports, or legal beats. And everyone learned to talk to the rotary press as though it were an old nag you had to urge on to the finish line. It goes without saying that, with such limited human capital, "no absence could be taken lightly." So it was that the dedicated scriptor worked through the day and night of Baby M.'s birth, signing both of the next day's editorials.

Just as we can understand the Englishman George Lesley's reticence regarding the thirteenth train without making judgements about human projections, beliefs, and superstitions, so can we also appreciate the parallel between the length of *l'Évangéline*'s life and that of Jesus Christ's stay on this earth: thirty-three years. An Acadian numerologist would have a heyday. Further interpretative adventures might be undertaken on the parallel roles of *l'Évangéline* and of DNA in preserving heredity, or on the consistency of double numbers reflected in the number thirty-three, the double nature of Jesus Christ (both God and man), and the double helix of the DNA molecule. Of course, this list of potential comparisons is by no means exhaustive. Once you get started, parallels, like railroad tracks, are almost without end. Furthermore, in addition to being the basis of the rail industry, the parallel is also the basis of cinematographic film, whose repercussions on humanity have equalled those of the railway. As for parallelism in writing, it goes back further than one or two centuries. We need only look to the Holy Scriptures, and more specifically to the parables of Jesus Christ, which are essentially comparisons, that is, operations drawing parallels between one thing and another. Of course, in the case of the parables, it must be said that long deep thought is often required to understand Christ's intended meaning. Some would require a lifetime of reflection. Unless one is a novelist, it's best not to worry too much about these. Excessive guilt hampers the work of repair, even when we don't know what exactly is broken.

☙

Élizabeth is seated at a small table on a sun-drenched terrace on the isle of Corfu. She has finally seen the famed serpent-haired Medusa, which in this place has been transformed into a mythological monster symbolizing "the perversion of spiritual and progressive impulses into vain stagnation." Élizabeth wanted to see with her own eyes this figure that also embodies the caduceus, the universal symbol of medical science. She decided to take this voyage on her last trip to Montréal, after her meeting with Brigitte, and before starting back to Moncton. As she turned off the sunny avenue onto a side street, her gaze had fallen on the large posters of Greece in the window of a travel agency. She had only briefly hesitated before stepping through the doorway. In the end, she had completely forgotten her appointment at the hairdressers.

The caduceus, "most ancient of symbols," portraying "a staff around which two serpents are coiled in opposite directions," illustrates the equilibrium achieved by the integration of opposing forces. In the chronicled history of civilizations, the staff represents "the axis around which the world turns," referred to sometimes as the cosmic pillar, the tree of life, the erect phallus, or the spinal column; the column of a temple or a column of light, or then again the sceptre, symbol of "the spirit's dominion over the body." The serpent alone, symbol of "the primordial undifferentiated, reservoir of all latency . . . playing on the sexes as it plays on all opposites," represents all complementary principles: the soul and the libido, the womb and the phallus, movement and water, the diurnal and the nocturnal, good and evil, sulphur and mercury, fixedness and volatility, the damp and the dry, hot and cold, left and right. The legend of the caduceus therefore comes from the "primordial chaos (two serpents fighting) and its polarization (separation of the serpents by Hermes), with their eventual entwinement around the staff, thus achieving the equilibrium of opposite tendencies around the axis of the world." A variation on this interpretation emphasizes the snake's vain nature, so that the coiling around the cosmic pillar represents "vanity tamed and submissive," transforming the serpent's venom into medicine, hence the art of Asclepius, father and future god of medicine, who "employed poisons to cure the sick and revive the dead." As the emblem of Hermes, messenger of the gods and guide to the living in their transformations, the caduceus became the ideal symbol for psychosomatic equilibrium because it represents "the even hand, the harmonization of desires . . . the ordering of affectivity, the need for spiritual-sublimation, [which] not only rules over the health of the soul [but] codetermines the health of the body." From a yogic point of view, the caduceus around the waist of the ugly and apparently insane Medusa (mouth wide open, eyes bulging, and the less-than-reassuring serpents in her hair) illustrates the disorder which threatens those who are unawakened to the cosmic consciousness and who, consequently, seek nourishment in distorted images of themselves.

Her head resting against the back of her chair, Élizabeth offers her face up to the sun, shutting her eyes for a moment on human myths and beliefs. The *Dictionnaire des symboles*, written by Jean Chevalier and Alain Gheerbrant, lies on the table beside the plate in which a few olive pits swim in a pool of oil and basil. Funny to find herself in Greece with this book under her arm, she who has always shunned mythology, with its countless figures butting into life whenever they please, without regard for whether they are real people or imaginary creatures. She smiles too because of the heat on her face and the light which illuminates everything. In this light that fosters exquisite daydreams, Élizabeth imagines Claude magically appearing, he stunned to find her here, while she accepts it as a natural unfolding. They would gaze at each other a long time in the abundant light, occasionally speaking but barely, because once again there is the unfathomable and the unspeakable.

But Élizabeth is suddenly jolted from her half-sleep by a passer-by bumping her table on his way to another. Not Claude. This is another man, who excuses himself, but not too much. Just enough to ask if he can join her. Élizabeth points to a chair. The man spots the *Dictionnaire des symboles* on the table and risks commenting, in an accent Élizabeth does not recognize, that she "is taking it seriously." He says he has never been fascinated by symbols but, if necessary, he can manage to find anything interesting. Then, in a confidential tone and at the risk, he admits, of appearing slightly odd, he confides that "doing whatever is necessary" is what he enjoys most. Élizabeth wonders if she is really hearing what she thinks she is hearing. She suspects that a slap is in order, but she finds herself unable to disregard the man's soft eyes and innocent smile. She thinks of the caduceus's equilibrium of opposites, wonders if she has fallen into some sort of tourist trap or into a true moment of cosmic magic; into a good book (. . . and they loved each other forever and ever and ever) or into a bad movie (. . . and they loved each other forever and ever and ever). She decides not to think about it too much and opts for the good book; if need be, she will write it.

Acknowledgements

Background information for this book has come from numerous sources. I have attempted to identify the principal ones in the course of the story itself, namely Roland Barthes, author of *Writing Degree Zero* (Jonathan Cape Ltd., 1967); Françoise Dolto, author of *Solitude* (Gallimard, 1994); Jean Chevalier and Alain Gheerbrant, authors of the *Dictionnaire des symboles* (Robert Laffont/Jupiter, 1982); Jean Chastenet, author of *Winston Churchill et l'Angleterre du XXe siècle* (Librairie Arthème Fayard, 1956); and Kjell Espmark, author of *Le Prix Nobel* (Éditions Balland, 1986). However, in wanting to avoid weighing down the story with many footnotes and other customary references, I have not yet acknowledged other works which were also of great help. First and foremost, I am particularly indebted to all who contributed to the Acadian daily newspaper *l'Évangéline* from 1949 onward, and particularly in 1953. I am also indebted to the following: S.V. Haas and M.P. Haas, authors of *Management of Celiac Disease* (J.B. Lippincott Company, 1951); Michael Bloch, author of *The Secret File of the Duke of Windsor/ The Private Papers 1937–1972* (Harper & Row, 1988); Bernard S. Schlessinger and June H. Schlessinger, authors of *The Who's Who of Nobel Prize Winners, Second Edition* (The Oryx Press, 1990); Roger Boussinot, author of *L'Encyclopédie du cinéma* (Bordas, 1980); R.A.E. Pickard, author of the *Dictionary of 1,000 Best Films* (Associated Press, 1971); Nicholas Thomas, author of the *International Dictionary of Films and Film-makers, Directors, Actors and Actresses* (St. James Press, 1991); the Centrale catholique du cinéma, de la radio et de la télévision for its annual *Répertoire général des films*, and the Fédération des centres diocésains de cinéma for its *Index de 6,000 titres de films avec leur cote morale (1948–1955)*; *Time* magazine, August 24, 1953, edition, for its feature article on Alfred C. Kinsey, and for articles on George Jorgensen's sex transformation (December 15, 1952; April 20, 1953); and Paul Hofmann, author of *Cento Città/A Guide to the "Hundred Cities & Towns" of Italy* (Henry Holt and Company, 1988). Other works have also been very helpful, notably Grolier's *Le livre des connaissances*, *Le Grand Larousse*, and *le petit Robert 2*. I am also grateful to the Université de Moncton's Bibliothèque Champlain, for accessibility of information, and to the archives services of its Centre d'études acadiennes, where *l'Évangéline*'s "remains" are now kept. L'Hôpital Georges-L. Dumont's archives services also provided key information for this book.

Quotations on pp. 13, 14, 15, 17, 38, 39–40: from Roland Barthes, *Le degré zéro de l'écriture*, © Éditions du Seuil, Paris: 1953; *Writing Degree Zero*, translation by Annette Lavers and Colin Smith, Jonathan Cape Ltd.: 1967.

Quotations on pp. 21, 22, 24: from Françoise Dolto, *Solitude* © Éditions Gallimard, Paris: 1994.

Quotations on pp. 161, 162: from Jean Chevalier et Alain Gheerbrant, *Dictionnaire des symboles*, Robert Laffont/Jupiter, Paris: 1982, coll. «Bouquins».